ALSO BY JANE CUTLER

Family Dinner
with pictures by Philip Caswell

No Dogs Allowed
with pictures by
Tracey Campbell Pearson

MY WARTIME SUMMERS

MY

Wartime Summers

JANE CUTLER

FARRAR STRAUS GIROUX

NEW YORK

For Uncle Percy and Uncle Joe,
who went to war

———————————

Special thanks to my friend Clarence Cretan,
Captain, U.S.A.R., whose precise memory and
patient recollection of the war years made this book
possible.

Published simultaneously in Canada by HarperCollins*CanadaLtd*
Printed in the United States of America
Designed by Lilian Rosenstreich
First edition, 1994

Library of Congress Cataloging-in-Publication Data
Cutler, Jane.
My wartime summers / Jane Cutler. — 1st ed.
          p.   cm.
[1. World War, 1939–1945—United States—Fiction.]   I. Title.
PZ7.C985My   1994   [Fic]—dc20   94-9845   CIP   AC

1942

O N E

*I*t was the first day of summer vacation. Fifth grade and the terrible Miss Mackey were finally behind me, and I was stretched out on the couch on our screened-in porch, eating cinnamon toast and making up a radio show about the war.

The radio! We all loved the radio. And the people in the programs I faithfully listened to every week were as real to me as anyone I actually knew. Captain Midnight. Fibber McGee and Molly. Jack Armstrong, the All-American Boy, and the characters in Allen's Alley and in the fairy tales on "Let's Pretend." Every Saturday morning at ten, I bet, there wasn't a kid in the country who wasn't listening to that one. My friends and I even ate Cream of Wheat sometimes, out of loyalty to the program, since that was the sponsor.

In the story I was making up, I played all the characters, including the whole crew of a crippled bomber limping back to base with a motor blown off. I spoke everybody's lines and did the sound effects, too.

It was satisfying to get the plane safely back. And it was hard to have to send the weary crew out on another dangerous mission the very next day. But there was no choice.

The brave airmen understood, of course. "A new plane and a couple of hours' sleep, sir," I said in the pilot's honorable voice, "and we'll be ready for another run. Right, men?" "Right!" I answered in three different voices, one after another. In a fourth voice, the commander's, I praised the men for their courage, and I wished them luck. Then, to end the program, I imitated the thump of enemy artillery in the background and said in the deep voice of the announcer: "But there was a problem the pilot didn't know about: there was no new plane available for the next day's mission. They would have to fly in the same one, whether it could be fixed perfectly or not! Tune in tomorrow for the further adventures of 'A Bomber Called Lucky.' "

Just as I was starting to work on the next episode, my friend Eddie opened the screen door and stuck his head in. His summer haircut was so short it made him look almost bald. "Ellen! There's strangers—maybe Germans!—in front of Mrs. Anger's. Come on!"

I jumped up. Germans at Mrs. Anger's! Eddie and I cut through some neighbors' yards, scrambled over our friend Marvin's fence, and crept behind the low bushes that separated Marvin's driveway from Mrs. Anger's.

Out on the sidewalk, underneath the leafy branches of a maple tree, stood the strangers: a man, a woman, and a girl about our age. They were wearing dark clothes and carrying winter coats. Three small suitcases were on the sidewalk at their feet.

"Listen!" Eddie whispered.

The man and the woman were studying a piece of paper and talking. I couldn't make out what they were saying, but I could hear enough to know that they were saying it in a different language.

"German!" I mouthed to Eddie. He nodded, looking serious.

My heart pounded. In my head, I heard the honorable pilot's voice. "Yes, sir," he said. "We can take them, sir."

"Are you sure?" asked the commander.

"I'm sure," the pilot answered. "We have surprise on our side, sir. And English."

I tensed, getting ready to move. But Eddie knew me pretty well. He'd been there nearly every time I'd gotten myself into trouble, from kindergarten on. Just as I was about to cry "Geronimo!," leap over the bushes, and capture the Germans, he put out his arm. "Stay down, Ellen," he whispered. "Don't do *anything.*"

As if his puny arm could keep me from my patriotic duty!

"Geronimo!" I cried, jumping over the shrubs and rushing at the startled strangers. Without any real plan in my mind, I grabbed the girl. I threw my arm around her neck so she couldn't move and then twisted her wrist behind her. It was a judo hold that Eddie's older brother, Dan, had taught me, after he used it on me once.

"Papa!" the girl screamed.

"Ellen!" Eddie cried, standing straight up in alarm.

"*Mein Gott!*" shrieked the woman, putting both hands up to her face.

"*Lass das!*" yelled the man, swatting at me with the piece of paper. "Stop what you are doing!"

"Let go, Ellen," Eddie hollered. "Let go!" Out of the corner of my eye, I saw his pale, scared face. Then I saw the flash of his skinny legs as he took off.

"*Hilfe!*" sobbed the woman. "Help!"

"Papa!" cried the girl.

Suddenly I came to my senses. I let go of the girl and backed away. Then I turned and tore off after Eddie, running for dear life.

I skidded into our secret headquarters, the toolshed over at Eddie's, right behind him. Marvin was there, sitting with his back up against the wall and his nose in an old *Superman* comic book. Dan was there, too, softening his Rawlings baseball mitt with oil. Both of them looked up as we came in the door.

"Germans!" I gasped. "Two grownups and a little girl, over at Mrs. Anger's!"

Marvin looked pleased. "A German girl," he said. "That's great! Now we'll have someone to be the enemy when we play war."

1942

"Really great," Eddie said. "Ellen went and attacked them already."

"She did?" Marvin turned his eager face to me. "You attacked three Germans?"

"No I did not!"

"Yes you did too!" Eddie insisted.

"I did not attack three Germans! I attacked one!"

"Which one?" inquired Dan.

"The kid, of course," I told him.

"You are really dumb, Ellen," Dan said mildly.

Dan always acted so superior. I wanted to sock him. "We don't even know for sure they're Germans," I told him, trying to wriggle out of the blame.

"I hope they are," Marvin persisted, "so we'll have someone to be the German when we play."

"She might not want to be," Dan pointed out, pounding his fist into his mitt.

"It won't matter," Marvin said. "If she's a German, then she'll have to be."

"If she's German," Eddie said, squinching his eyes thoughtfully, "she might be a spy."

"A child spy?" Marvin wondered.

"Her parents, dum-dum," I said, flopping down onto the one rickety chair and crossing my eyes at him.

"They're not spies," Dan informed us. "They're refugees."

"What are refugees?" asked Marvin.

"People who have to run away from Hitler so they won't get killed," said Dan.

"Oh, sure," said Eddie. "How do you know that?"

"Know what?" asked Dan.

"That they're refugees? That they're not German?"

"They are German, stupid. They're German and they're refugees. And they're going to live in that apartment Mrs. Anger made in her basement."

Dan always managed to know what was going on before the rest of us did. It was infuriating.

"My dad says that apartment is illegal," said Marvin.

"So what if it is?" asked Dan. "There's a housing shortage, don't you know? New people have to live someplace."

"Yeah," Eddie chimed in. "There's a war on, Marv. Remember?"

Eddie pulled the comic away from Marvin and Marvin tried to get it back. But he was afraid of Eddie, and he ended up looking at it over Eddie's shoulder. Dan spread more oil onto his mitt.

"If they're German," I insisted, "then I bet they *are* spies. Spies pretending to be refugees."

"Spies don't travel around in families, Ellen," Dan informed me. "Spies don't come with a kid to live in Mrs. Anger's basement."

"You don't know," I argued. "You don't know anything about spies. You're a moron!"

"You're afraid if those people are refugees instead of spies, you're going to get in big trouble for attacking their little girl," Dan said. "You're the moron."

"Yeah," said Eddie, looking up from *Superman*, "you are."

"Are what?" I demanded angrily.

"Going to be in trouble," Eddie said.

TWO

I hung around the tool-shed until the others left. Then I took the long way home. And dawdled. I expected the worst.

"Wash up and then set the table, Ellen," my mother called when she heard me come in. "Daddy and Uncle Bob will be home from work any minute."

Uncle Bob was my dad's younger brother, and he lived with us. He always had, since their parents both died when he was just a little kid. He got here even before I did, more than eleven years ago.

I ran the water in the bathroom sink and wet the palms of my hands. Then I wiped the dirt off on a towel.

"If we have to bail out over enemy territory," the pilot said to his crew, "it will be curtains for us."

"What'll they do to us?" asked the tail gunner.

"We can't know for sure," the pilot told him. "But

if we fall into enemy hands, it could mean—a firing squad!"

The tail gunner made a scared sound, like someone had just hit him in the stomach.

"Ellen?" my mother called.

I ditched the towel in the laundry hamper and went into the kitchen.

"What's for supper?" I asked, trying to sound perfectly calm, watching my mother to see if she knew anything yet.

"Macaroni-and-cheese and green beans and Jell-O salad," she answered, putting some bread on a plate and handing it to me to put on the kitchen table.

I set the bread down and got out the silverware, the blue plates, and the glasses.

"Napkins," my mother reminded me.

I got out the napkins. Clearly, she hadn't heard. This puzzled me. It wasn't like Mrs. Anger not to call up about every little thing, let alone something serious. Maybe the Germans hadn't told her yet. Maybe they weren't going to tell her. If they were spies, they might not want to make a fuss or call extra attention to themselves. "Let them be spies," I prayed. "Please let them be spies, and I'll never do anything stupid again as long as I live."

"Ellen"—my mother gave me a little push—"don't just stand there daydreaming, honey. You know your father likes to eat as soon as he gets home."

My father and Uncle Bob worked together at my father's locksmith shop. Uncle Bob had helped my dad on Saturdays until he graduated from high school. Then he went full time. If it hadn't been for the war, Uncle Bob said, he might have thought about doing something different. But he figured until he got drafted, he'd just as soon be a locksmith. He and my dad went downtown together in the morning, both of them climbing into the front of Daddy's Buick. They came home together in the evening, washed up together, and sat down at the table together.

Tonight, when they came in, they were talking about the usual thing: whether Uncle Bob should wait to be drafted or whether he should enlist.

My dad was all for Uncle Bob enlisting, in the Navy. "It's a cleaner life, Bob," Daddy was saying, probably for about the millionth time. "Everything's spit and polish on a ship. None of this crawling around in the dirt and living down in a hole.

"It's what I'd do, I can tell you," Daddy said.

My dad wasn't going to be able to join the Navy, or the Army, either. Or the Marines. He was 4-F. Blind in one eye. He and Bob had cooked up a scheme to try to get him into the service. My dad borrowed an eye chart from the optometrist's office and memorized it until he could recite the letters perfectly with one hand over his good eye. Then he went down to enlist in the Navy.

But it didn't work. The Navy used different eye charts, and switched them around. You'd think they had to guard against a lot of half-blind old guys like my father trying to get in, when my mother insisted that my dad was crazy, and the only one his age—he was a whole lot older than Uncle Bob—who would want to put himself in harm's way.

"What do you mean, my age?" Daddy had asked when she said that.

"Just what I said." Mom had stood right up to him that time. "A man in his middle thirties with a wife and a child is not going to be drafted. So it doesn't make sense for you to be trying to join when they don't really need you anyway."

I noticed Mom didn't mention the blind part when she argued with my father about his trying to enlist. Mom wasn't like me. She didn't have a mean bone in her body.

Daddy and Uncle Bob and I sat down and put our napkins on our laps. Mom got the food out and poured iced coffee for the grownups and a glass of milk for me.

Daddy was stubborn. "In the Navy, you've got your own bunk, clean and dry," he reminded Uncle Bob. "You've got everything organized. You've got a bathroom and a shower. I can't understand why you'd wait around to get drafted into the Army when you could go right down there and join the Navy tomorrow morning if you wanted to."

"He doesn't want to be in the Navy, Daddy," I said, forgetting for a moment that I was already in danger and that arguing with my father was not going to make things easier for me.

Mom jumped in. "Bob wants to go to Europe, Frank," she said, "you know that. He wants to fight against the Germans, not the Japanese. If he joins the Navy, he might get sent to the wrong part of the war."

She passed the Jell-O salad to my dad.

1942

"Right," Uncle Bob said. "Hitler's the one I want to get. Pass the beans, please." I passed the bowl of green beans. "Germans, right, Ellen?" Uncle Bob winked at me. "They're the ones, right?"

That wink. What did it mean? Had Uncle Bob somehow found out about my attacking the German girl?

Just then the telephone rang, and I jumped about a mile and knocked over my milk. Daddy went to get the phone, and Mom grabbed a couple of towels to wipe up with. Bob made his face all innocent and looked dopily around the kitchen, saying, "Where's the mop? Has anybody seen the mop?" Then he took hold of my hair. "Oh, never mind," he said. "Here it is. I found it."

By the time my dad came back to the table, Uncle Bob had helped me clean up the milk and poured a fresh glass for me, and Mom had set out a big bowl of strawberries and a pitcher of cream, for dessert.

"That was Flora Lefkowitz, Rosemary," Dad told my mother. Marvin's mom! "I said you'd call her back."

It wasn't usual for neighbors to call up on the telephone. Most of the time, they would just come over. "Do you know what it was about?" my mother asked.

"She said there's a German refugee family moved into Mrs. Anger's." I choked on the new milk and started to cough. Bob pounded me on the back.

"German refugees?" my mother asked. "From Germany?"

"Jews," my father explained. "Germans who believe in the Jewish religion. Hitler doesn't like them."

My mother looked puzzled. "But if they're Germans . . ."

"Doesn't matter," my father told her. "He kills them anyway."

"See?" said Uncle Bob. "I told you, Hitler's the one to get!"

We moved into the living room. Daddy read the paper, Uncle Bob and I played checkers, and Mom cleaned the kitchen and then went to call Mrs. Lefkowitz. I strained to hear, and Uncle Bob jumped both my kings. "You're not paying attention, Ellen," he warned happily, stacking the red checkers on his side of the board.

"Line's busy," Mom reported as she sat down in the wing chair and took out her knitting.

It turned out to be a nice evening. Apparently nobody knew about the attack—at least not yet. I breathed a sigh of relief. If the Germans hadn't told on me by now, maybe they weren't going to.

Uncle Bob and I played until "The Shadow" came on the radio. Then we stopped. It was one of our favorite programs, and we wanted to hear every word. "Who knows what evil lurks in the hearts of men?" said the eerie voice at the beginning. "The Shadow knows!"

"That's all right with me," I thought to myself. "As long as he doesn't call my parents."

It was a good joke, and I wished I could tell it to someone. But I couldn't take the chance. Even Uncle Bob might not understand if he found out that I'd attacked the new girl for no reason at all.

THREE

*T*he next morning, I was the first kid out. It was quiet, warm already and on its way to hot. I looked around at the duplexes and the three-story apartment buildings and the single-family houses like ours. I looked at the perfect lawns and the scruffy ones and at the tall trees that marched up one side of the street and back down the other. Nobody was in sight. So I waited, poking a stick into a bare spot on our lawn, where the grass wasn't growing.

I tried to guess who would come out next. Maybe Eddie. Or Marvin. Or Dan. Or the new girl. What if she was the first one out? What would I do?

It was Eddie, with his arms still streaked with dirt from yesterday and sleep in the corners of his eyes, barefoot and cranky and munching on a piece of toast. He sat down next to me on the lawn. "What happened last night?" he asked.

"Nothing," I told him.

"Nothing?"

I shook my head. "Nothing."

"Mrs. Anger didn't call your parents?"

"Nope."

"Something funny's going on," he said thoughtfully.

"I guess the Germans didn't tell."

"I guess they didn't," Eddie said. "The question is why they didn't."

I shrugged.

"If they didn't tell, they're spies for sure," Eddie reasoned.

"No," I said, "they aren't. They're Jews."

"Jews? What does that have to do with anything? Marvin's a Jew."

"If they're Jews, they can't be spies."

"Who says?" Eddie wanted to know.

"I say."

"What makes you so sure all of a sudden?"

"My father explained it to me," I told him. "They're Germans *and* they're Jews. And that's how come they're refugees. Because Hitler is trying to kill off all the Jews, even his own German ones. Don't ask me why."

"They could just be saying they're Jews and really be Germans and not Jews. And really be spies," Eddie said. "I bet that's it. I bet they're pretending to be Jews so they can spy and find out all our secrets and send them back to Germany. In code. They probably have a code machine set up in their apartment already. Bet?"

"What secrets?" I asked. I hated arguing with Eddie. Once he got an idea in his head, it just stuck there. Now he didn't bother to answer. He was thinking, whistling through his teeth and wriggling his toes impatiently.

"Just secrets," he said finally. "Whatever they can find out."

We sat there, waiting for the day to start. I poked and poked at the bare spot, making it worse, and Eddie squinted into the distance and chewed on a blade of grass.

After a while I saw the new girl come slowly up the stairs from Mrs. Anger's basement and start toward us. She walked as if she wasn't going anywhere in particular. Eddie and I watched her.

The girl was wearing a pink-and-white-checked pinafore. Her curly dark brown hair was held back off her face with a ribbon. When she got close to where we were sitting, she stooped down and pretended to be looking at some flowers growing near the sidewalk. But I have eyes like a hawk, and I saw her glance over at us.

"Hey!" I called.

She stood up and looked at me, but she didn't answer.

"Can you speak English?" Eddie yelled.

She came a couple of steps closer. From the way she was studying Eddie and me, I realized she wasn't sure whether or not we were the two from yesterday. After all, I'd been behind her, and Eddie had taken off.

"Can you speak English?" Eddie asked again. She sat down on the grass a few feet away from us.

"I speak English. Some," she answered.

"You're going to get grass stains on that pinafore," I said, wanting her to understand that she was too dressed up for a summer morning in the middle of America.

"Yes," she agreed.

"You're a German, aren't you?" Eddie asked.

She shook her head yes.

"We shouldn't be talking to you, then," he told her. She frowned. "Why?"

"Because you could be a German spy," he said. "You could be here spying on us and undermining the war effort. You could be here finding out all about us and sending secret code messages back to Hitler. That's why."

The girl giggled. "Hitler?" she said. "Do you think Hitler will care to know any things about you?"

"He might!" I said, backing Eddie up.

She shook her head and tried not to laugh again. "I can promise to you," she told us, "Hitler does not think about you. Not at all. And I and my parents are not a spy."

"Spies," I corrected.

"Yes," she said, "I and my parents are not spies."

Just then Marvin and Dan came around the corner of the garage, firing machine guns at the top of their lungs. Eddie and I ran for cover, bent over double, as soon as we heard them. We dove behind the forsythias and waited until they were within range before we opened up. As soon as we began to fire, the two of them hit the dirt. The German girl sat right where she was.

1942

We fired back and forth for a while, and then Eddie and I stopped. Dan jumped up and tried to storm the forsythias. He must have thought we were out of ammunition. That was just what we wanted him to think. "You fell for it!" Eddie cried, standing up and blazing away again.

He and Dan fired point-blank at each other until they both fell over dead. I sat tight and waited for Marvin. But he didn't come. After about a minute of nothing happening, I peered around the edge of the forsythia. Marvin was sitting on the grass talking to the new girl.

"Lefkowitz," I yelled impatiently, "are you playing or not?"

"I'm not," Marvin called.

Eddie lifted his head. So did Dan. But Marvin really wasn't paying any attention, so they got up and brushed the grass and dirt off their clothes and went and sat down next to Marvin and the girl.

"I won, then," I called, "and the four of you are my prisoners. Hands in the air!"

"No," the girl said. "I don't play games from war. My mother does not allow it."

"And I'm dead," said Dan.

"And I'm on your side. And dead, too," said Eddie.

Marvin stood up and put his hands in the air. I came out from behind the forsythia and approached him. "Name, rank, and serial number, soldier," I demanded.

"Marvin Lefkowitz," Marvin said. "Four-star general. And I forgot my serial number."

"Which army are you with, General?" I asked roughly, keeping him covered.

"Allied army. And that's all I'm going to tell you."

"Allied army? That's a lie! Eddie and I are the Allied army. We're the American Army, if you want to know."

"Well . . ." Marvin hesitated.

"We're the British," Dan said.

"So who's the German?" I asked.

Marvin pointed to the new girl. "She's the German," he said. "But her mother won't let her play."

"Halitosis!" I swore. "This is ridiculous. The Allied Forces have been fighting each other."

"Again," said Eddie.

"Again," I agreed. "We really need to get this war better organized, like the real one is."

The boys nodded. Then we all just sat there.

"I am Lisa-Lotte," the girl said at last. "Lisa-Lotte Siegel. I and my parents came from New York on a train. Before that, on a ship, from Europe. Perhaps you would like to know, my father has one time stood this close to Hitler." She held her hands about a foot apart.

"Your father saw Hitler?" I asked.

"Up close to himself," Lisa-Lotte Siegel answered, "on a train."

"He was up close to Hitler on a train?" asked Marvin. "What about all the guards around Hitler? How did your father get that close?"

Lisa-Lotte frowned and spoke carefully. "It was not my father to get close to Hitler," she explained. "It was Hitler to get close to my father."

She looked from one of us to another. Then she tried again. "My father—is on a train. He goes to the mountains in order to ski. And Hitler, he is on the same train. And he passes so closely to my father, if my father has had a gun, he could have shot him."

"He didn't have a gun! Oh, no!" Eddie cried, slapping himself on the forehead and falling over backwards. "He didn't have a gun!"

"Of course he does not," Lisa-Lotte said firmly. "Why would my father have with him a gun to go to the mountains? My father has with him his skis."

"He should have bonked Hitler over the head with his skis," Marvin said.

"It is not my father's fault," Lisa-Lotte said. "It is a long time before. Before Hitler is Hitler. Before my father knows. Before anyone knows. My father is so young, he does not yet to meet my mother!"

We were all quiet then. I don't know what the boys were thinking. But I was remembering the small, nervous-looking man from yesterday. I was trying to imagine him doing something as daring as skiing.

Just then, from down the block, from the steps leading to Mrs. Anger's basement, came a strangled-sounding cry, "Lisa-Lotte! Lisa-Lotte! Come!"

It was Lisa-Lotte's mother, calling her in. Lisa-Lotte jumped up and left. The rest of us just sat there, surprised to hear anyone sounding like that, feeling frightened by the sound of her frightened voice.

FOUR

*U*ncle Bob was 1-A, not 4-F like my father, and he got drafted into the Army. He had to go to Texas for basic training, and they gave him less than a week to get ready.

"Texas!" my mother exclaimed, as if he were being sent to Mars. "Texas! With all the Army bases right here in the Midwest, why in the world are they sending you all the way to Texas?"

"Mine is not to reason why," Uncle Bob declared, "mine is but to do or die!"

"That's the Army for you," Daddy said. "They make you take the longest way from point A to point B any time they can."

"There's so many soldiers," I reminded him, "they can't make it easy for everybody."

"You're the only one I know who makes good

sense!" Uncle Bob said, picking me up and turning me around above his head, like a propeller on a plane.

"Put me down!" I screeched happily.

"Never!"

"Put me down!"

When he did, I pretended to be too dizzy to stand, and I fell over onto the couch.

"That's what I'm going to do to the enemy!" Uncle Bob cried, pushing me up and down on the sofa cushions. "Say uncle," he commanded.

"Uncle!"

"Say 'Uncle Bob'!"

"Uncle Bob!"

He quit torturing me and sat down on the couch, stretching his extra-long legs out in front of him. "That's how we're going to win the war," he said. "Twirl them till they're too dizzy to fight and then make them say uncle."

My mother shook her head. "I have two children, not one," she said.

Uncle Bob jumped to his feet and started to pick her up. "Robert Parker, don't you dare!" she said, laughing.

"I don't know, Bobby," my father said, looking up at his brother, "I just do not know. Do you think they're going to let you get away with your high jinks in the U.S. Army?"

Most of Uncle Bob's friends had girls they liked, and as soon as they were drafted, they got engaged. Mike Brooks even got married! But Uncle Bob didn't have a girlfriend. He had one once, in high school, but she threw him over for someone in the service. "It's the uniform, Bobby," my father told him at the time, trying to make him feel better. "A girl can't resist a man in uniform."

It was true. I loved to see soldiers and sailors in their uniforms. Every single one of them looked handsome. I bet even Eddie would look good in a uniform.

Anyway, because Uncle Bob didn't have a girl, he didn't have anyone special to say goodbye to. Just us. So the night before he left, he was home.

Mom made his favorite supper, meat loaf and peas and mashed potatoes and gravy. When we finished eating, Uncle Bob and I helped her do the dishes while Daddy watered the lawn. And after that, we all piled into the Buick and headed for the Premium Dairy Fountain to get ice cream.

For once, my parents sat in the back seat. Uncle Bob drove, and I sat up front next to him. I pretended that Uncle Bob was the pilot and I was the copilot of a B-17 bomber. My parents were the bombardier and the tail gunner. We were setting off on another episode of "A Bomber Called Lucky," hoping that the engine, which was hanging on to the wing by a thread, sort of like a loose tooth, would stay on until we carried out our mission and made it safely back. With Robert Parker and Ellen Parker up front at the controls, there was a good chance we could pull it off. There was no moon, and the road ahead of us was dark. Hopefully, the enemy would have a hard time spotting us.

1942

As we approached the dairy, I said, "Target straight ahead, sir," to Uncle Bob.

"I see it," he answered. "What's this 'sir' business?"

I felt my face turn red. "Nothing," I mumbled.

We parked next to the big, circular basin with the fountain in the middle at exactly the right moment. The water was down, so we had time to give the carhop our order and settle in before it started up again.

"I don't know why this is always fun to watch," Mom said. "I bet we've seen it a million times."

"Two million," Daddy said. He was staring moodily out the open window of the car, smoking a cigarette.

I started to say that I thought it would be fun to watch the fountain even if we'd seen it ten million times, but just then Uncle Bob said, "There she goes!"

The first spurt of the water was low and soft, sort of like the bubbler in the drinking fountain at the park. The second spurt was higher, and the third was even higher. By the time the water rose up out of the center of the basin for the fourth and last time, turning green and blue and pink and lavender as the lights hidden under the basin's rim shone on it, it towered over everything.

I felt the way I always felt, watching the column of water change from one color to another, watching it stay up and stay up. I felt hopeful, just like some little kid who didn't know better, that it wouldn't come down again.

Suddenly the column of water collapsed.

I let out my breath and took a sip of the root beer float Uncle Bob had passed over to me. But I kept my eyes glued on the center of the pool, waiting for the whole beautiful thing to begin again.

On the way home, Mom said, "I don't understand how we can find that fountain so satisfying to watch, every single time."

"I think it's knowing exactly what's going to happen," Uncle Bob said. "Anticipating." He drove with his elbow out of the open window and only one hand on the steering wheel.

"It's knowing that it's going to keep going, over and over again," I said, "but thinking that it might not."

"There's certainly something hypnotic about it," Mom added.

"And it's pretty," said Uncle Bob.

"Drive with both hands, would you, Bob?" was all my father said.

Uncle Bob left the next morning, and we started getting letters from him almost right away. "I didn't think Bob would be a letter writer," Mom said. "Maybe he's homesick."

The first letter didn't tell us much we didn't already know. He got to Texas, which he said was hotter than Hades, and dusty, and dry. He had his hair practically shaved off and he got a bunch of shots. He slept on a cot in a big barracks with about fifty other GIs. And he was assigned to KP, which meant he had to peel tons of potatoes and clean latrines.

1942

I knew all of this stuff already, from watching the newsreels at the movies, where I went with my friends on Saturday afternoons. "America Goes to War," the announcer's voice would say, and then they'd show GIs in basic training. They'd show planes taking off from the decks of aircraft carriers. They'd show Princess Elizabeth and her sister, Princess Margaret, standing out on the balcony of their palace in England, waving and smiling. Even though they knew Hitler might be getting ready to take over England any minute, they kept waving and smiling.

So nothing Uncle Bob told us about his basic training in Texas was news, and the only thing that made it interesting was that now it was happening to him.

I was proud of Uncle Bob, and I was sure he'd be a hero and get medals. Maybe he'd be the one to capture Hitler, not miss the chance the way Lisa-Lotte's father had.

When I told Mom I thought Uncle Bob was going to come home a hero, she said, "Let's just pray that he comes home in one piece."

If Daddy and Uncle Bob had gone together, the two of them could have been heroes. I could see us at the White House, watching the ceremony.

"Hero medals for both of you," President Franklin Delano Roosevelt was saying, "for outstanding bravery, and for capturing Adolf Hitler and bringing him back alive." The President pinned a huge, shiny medal onto my father's chest and another one onto Uncle Bob's. Then he shook hands with them and the Marine band began to play. "And to think," the President exclaimed to my father, "that you were able to perform above and beyond the call of duty with only one good eye! I congratulate you!''

"Thank you, President Roosevelt, sir,'' my father answered quietly. "There's not a man I know wouldn't do the same.''

"The Army is all hurry-up-and-wait,'' wrote Uncle Bob. "We stand in line for everything. I am meeting men from all parts of the country and from all walks of life. I am glad to have good buddies. You are nothing in the Army without buddies.

"One of the first things you find out is what SNAFU means. It means 'Situation Normal, All Fouled Up.' That really is the Army for you.''

"I told him to join the Navy,'' Daddy said.

"They get us up at 5:30 a.m. every day,'' Uncle Bob wrote, "and they keep us going for fifteen hours and more. If they show a training film in the evening, I fall asleep the minute they turn off the lights. We all do.

"They made me learn how to take apart my rifle and put it back together while I was blindfolded. I wonder if they are going to make me fight wearing a blindfold (ha-ha!).

"So how are things back there?'' he wrote. "Civilian life seems far away.''

I was back in school by the time Uncle Bob finished his ninety days of basic training and got a furlough. He had one week off before he had to report to Communications School, where he was going to learn to be a radio operator.

1942

When I first found out about this, I thought it meant he was going to broadcast radio programs for the soldiers to listen to. But my dad explained that Uncle Bob was going to learn how to operate the radios they used to communicate from the front lines to the rear and from one part of a battle to another. Bob was going to have to go into battle carrying his rifle and ammunition, his heavy pack, and a radio set, too.

When Uncle Bob first walked in wearing his uniform, I felt shy. But as soon as he put on the clothes he called his "civvies," his regular old pants and shirt, I could see he hadn't really changed.

Mom seemed to think he had. "Bobby," she told him, "I hardly know you, you're that different-looking."

"Uglier," Daddy said, winking at me.

"Not a bit," Mom protested. "Handsomer!"

"Now, Rosie," Uncle Bob teased, "how could I be handsomer? I was the handsomest man in town to start with!"

Uncle Bob slept a lot that week. And he ate like a horse, Mom said. He had a long walk and a talk with my father on Saturday afternoon. And on Saturday night, he went out with the friends he had who were still around, and he came home drunk. Drunk! I couldn't believe it. He was so noisy, coming in, he woke us all up. And then he puked.

I thought Daddy would give Uncle Bob what-for the next day. It was late by the time he came down and hunched over a cup of black coffee instead of eating breakfast.

I hung around in the kitchen, not wanting to miss a thing. But all my father said was "I guess the Army's made a man out of you, Bobby."

And all Uncle Bob said back was "I guess it has."

And that was that.

Later, in the afternoon, Uncle Bob climbed into his uniform again and got ready to go. Communications School would keep him in Texas another ten weeks, he told me. Then he'd be shipped overseas, but he didn't know where.

I had the feeling he really did know, and that he just wasn't supposed to tell.

"You can tell me," I wheedled. "I can keep a secret."

Uncle Bob whooped. "Since when?"

"Since you've been away," I fibbed.

"Really?" he asked. "Honest?"

"Cross my heart and hope to die," I told him, "no fingers crossed." I held out both hands for him to see.

"Well then, you come over here, and I'll tell you. But you have to promise me you won't breathe it to a living soul. This is serious, Ellen. This is war."

I promised.

Uncle Bob looked around. He put his finger to his lips and pointed out the door. I followed him onto the sidewalk in the front of the house and walked next to him while he paced.

"This way, nobody'll hear us," he said.

"Who would hear us in the house except Daddy and Mom?" I wanted to know.

1942

He frowned at me. "Loose lips sink ships," he scolded.

I giggled, but he didn't even smile. "I'm not sure I should be doing this," he said.

"Oh, please, Uncle Bob, please," I begged. "I won't tell. I promise." I looked up at him with my most honest face.

"Okay," he said. "I'll tell you. The secret. My assignment. First I'm going to Communications School." Pause. "Then I'm going overseas." Pause. "Either to Europe or"—pause—"to the Pacific."

I waited.

Uncle Bob laughed. "That's it! That's all I know. Tune in later for more up-to-the-minute news from the front!"

"Uncle Bob!" I threw myself at him, and we ended up wrestling on the lawn. "You lied to me!" I tried to pound his chest, but he held my wrists.

"Did not!"

"Did too!"

"Not!"

"Too!"

My mother pushed open the screen door. "Children!" she called. "Supper!"

I scrambled up. "Last one in is a rotten egg!" I cried, breaking for the house.

I heard Uncle Bob right behind me, and we made it to the doorway at exactly the same time and tried to squeeze through together.

"Good Lord!" my mother cried, backing up. "You two!"

FIVE

*U*ncle Bob's buddy Hal from basic training and Hal's brand-new wife, Jeanette, were coming through town. Hal was on his way to be trained as a glider pilot. The trip West was their honeymoon.

"The poor kids," my mother said. "Riding across the country on a crowded train is no kind of honeymoon."

"We didn't have a honeymoon," my father reminded her. "We survived."

Mom didn't say anything, and Daddy shook his head and went downtown to meet the train. Hal and Jeanette had a stopover, and they were coming all the way out to our house in the suburbs for supper.

Mom set up the drop-leaf table in the living room and got out a tablecloth and her good dishes.

"It's too hot to eat in the kitchen when I've had the

stove on all afternoon," she said. "Besides, if the poor kids can't have a honeymoon, they can at least have a nice meal to remember."

Hal and Jeanette were my first chance to study people in love. Outside of the movies, I'd never laid eyes on newlyweds before. I decided to take advantage of their visit and find out what I could about love. Information like that might come in handy.

Jeanette looked like a high-school girl. Her light brown hair was rolled up into a pompadour in the front and hung in waves down her back. She had on bright red lipstick and some of it had smeared onto her front teeth, which stuck out.

Hal was in uniform. Handsome.

Both Jeanette and Hal were shy. They answered questions in the shortest way they could. And they blushed when they talked. I wondered how they ever got to know each other well enough to get married. Maybe it was one of those hurry-up kind of marriages that my mother said were happening all over the country, because of the war.

"Did you and Hal get married in a big hurry?" I asked Jeanette when we sat down to eat.

Jeanette looked at her plate and blushed. "Sort of," she said.

"Because of the war?" I wanted to know.

"I guess," Jeanette whispered.

"If there wasn't a war, do you think you might have waited and gotten married to someone else?"

"Ellen!" my mother scolded, passing the chicken to Hal and frowning at me.

After dinner, we cleared the table and pushed it

back up against the wall so we could sit around in the living room and visit. Hal and Jeanette sat next to each other on the sofa, holding hands. Neither one of them spoke.

"So, Hal," my dad said, "how did you and Bob come to be friends?"

"We went through basic training together, sir," said Hal.

We know *that*, I thought.

"I mean, what brought you two together?" asked Daddy, doing his best.

"My bunk was next to Bob's, sir."

I sat on the hassock, watching carefully.

My father began to have trouble staying awake. Even my mother, who would talk about almost anything at all, didn't have any luck keeping this conversation going.

People in love don't talk much, I silently observed.

Daddy roused himself and tried again. "So," he said, "Hal."

"Sir?"

"You're going to be a glider pilot?"

"Yessir."

"Gliders," my mother said, sitting on the edge of her chair. "What are gliders, exactly?"

"Gliders are planes without engines, Mrs. Parker," Hal answered, looking at his shoes.

"What in the world do they do with planes that don't have engines?" Mom wondered.

"They're used to carry troops to the front, ma'am," said Hal.

1942

We all sat through another long silence. Then Mom turned to me. "Maybe Jeanette and Hal would like to see your room, Ellen," she said. "I bet they'd be interested in the crazy quilt you have that was your great-grandmother's. And they might want to look at the dollhouse you and Uncle Bob built."

If I hadn't been on my best behavior, which I was, since Uncle Bob had told us in his letters how important his buddies were to him, I would have choked myself with one hand and fallen to the floor gasping and kicking, to show Mom what I thought of her idea. But I *was* on my best behavior. And besides, Jeanette and Hal stood right up. They would love to see my room, Jeanette said.

So I trudged upstairs, with the two of them on my heels, holding hands and whispering.

"There's the quilt," I said, pointing to my bed. "And the dollhouse is in the closet."

Jeanette ran one finger around some of the pieces of material that made up the quilt pattern. "That's real pretty, Ellen," she said. Then she and Hal looked at the closed closet door. They wanted to see the dollhouse.

I shoved my roller skates and a blouse and some crumpled arithmetic papers off the top of the dollhouse and pulled it out for them.

Jeanette sat down on the floor, and Hal sat next to her. "Oh!" she said when she looked inside and saw the tiny cardboard furniture Uncle Bob and I had made and the family of dolls we'd bought to live in the dollhouse after we finished it.

Jeanette and Hal took out the mother and the father and the baby dolls. They took out the furniture. They set things up to suit themselves. They spoke to each other in whispers. Hal rubbed his chin on the top of Jeanette's head. They forgot I was there.

I sat with my back against the wall and watched. People in love are silly, I noted.

Jeanette and Hal gave the dolls a meal, sitting them around the kitchen table on the chairs Uncle Bob and I had made out of empty spools. They made the mother doll and the father doll hug and kiss a lot. And they made both of them rock the baby doll. Then they put the dolls to bed.

All this time, it was getting darker and darker in my room, and the only light, finally, was the streetlamp out under my window, shining in, like moonlight. Pretend moonlight to go with the pretend family in the pretend house.

When my father came to the door of my room to tell Hal and Jeanette it was time for him to take them back to the station, they jumped with surprise. Then they both got to their feet, acting more embarrassed than ever, and went on their way.

It was only a few weeks later when we heard from Jeanette again. She was at the station, waiting to change trains, she told my mom. She was calling to let us know that Hal was dead. Killed in a training accident. And she was on her way back home.

"Poor kid," Daddy said.

"Poor kids," Mom agreed.

"What a gyp!" I shook my head. "Killed before he even got to the war."

1942

Mom was shocked. "Ellen! What a coldhearted thing to say! I'm surprised at you."

Daddy went out on the back porch and stood there in the dark and smoked one cigarette after another, just the way he did when he got classified 4-F.

I imagined Hal's commanding officer stepping out of the shadows. "You'll have to take Hal's place," he said to my father. "There's no one else. Besides, you're more skilled flying with your one good eye than most of these younger men are with two."

"They've got other things on their minds, Colonel," my father said.

"Yeah," the colonel said, "I know. Love. They've got love on their minds. It distracts them. Makes them unlucky. We need grownup men to win the war, not boys in love. Are you with us, Parker?"

My father flipped his cigarette away and saluted. He was wearing a black patch over his bad eye. "I'm with you, sir. You know I am. But I'm classified as 4-F."

"You're about to be reclassified, as 1-A," promised the colonel. "Now, let's see about getting you trained as a glider pilot."

"Yes, sir!" said my father smartly.

I was glad Uncle Bob didn't have some girl on his mind. It would be awful for him to die in training, before he ever got a chance to fight. I mean, I guess you could say that Hal died for Democracy. But it wasn't the same.

When my father came back in, I said that to him. That it wasn't the same, somehow.

My father's answer surprised me. "Dead is dead,

Ellen," he said. And his steps going up the stairs were heavy and slow.

The morning my friends found out that Superman was 4-F, I was home fooling around with my radio sound effects kit. And by the time I went outside, everyone was sitting on Eddie's front steps, looking glum. I sat down and waited for somebody to tell me what was wrong.

"Superman is 4-F," Marvin said.

"Oh, sure, Marv," I answered.

"See for yourself." Dan handed me the *Superman* comic he was holding, the latest one, hot off the press.

I took it from him, but before I had a chance to open it, Eddie said, "Superman flunked the eye test."

"Flunked the eye test?" I asked. Now, this was interesting.

"It was his X-ray vision," Dan explained.

"He looked right through the wall," Marvin said.

"And read the eye chart in the next room," Eddie finished. Lisa-Lotte sighed.

"That's exactly what happened to my father!" I exclaimed. "That's why he's 4-F."

"Your father doesn't have X-ray vision, Ellen," sneered Eddie.

"He flunked the eye test, didn't he?"

"Yeah," Eddie allowed.

"And Superman flunked the eye test, too, right?"

"Yeah," Eddie said again.

"And that means they're both 4-F for exactly the same reason, doesn't it?"

Eddie hesitated. "Well . . ." he said.

"Doesn't it?" I insisted.

"I guess so," he said.

"For all you know, my father might be Superman," I said.

That was going too far. "Sure," said Dan, "Clark Kent *really* in disguise!"

I shoved Dan and he shoved me back. Then I settled down to read the comic. It was true, what they'd told me. I thought about my father. If Superman flunked the eye test and got classified 4-F, it was nothing to be so ashamed of. I couldn't wait for Daddy to get home from work, so I could tell him.

I met him at the door. "Daddy, guess what?" I said.

"Not now, Ellen," he answered, going to wash up and to change his shirt.

I waited until dinner was nearly over and tried again. "Daddy, guess what?"

"Ellen, you know I don't like guessing games," he said. "If you have something to say, just say it."

"Well, I just thought you'd like to know. Superman is 4-F."

"Superman?" My father frowned. He didn't approve of comic books. I wasn't allowed to have them in the house.

"He flunked the eye test, Daddy." Silence. "I just thought you should know."

"Superman is 4-F because he flunked the eye test," said my father. "And how did this important information happen to fall into your hands?"

I hated it when my father was sarcastic. "Daddy!" I protested.

"You know how your dad and I feel about comic

books, Ellen," my mother said. "You're not supposed to be reading them."

That wasn't quite true. They'd said I wasn't supposed to buy them, and I wasn't supposed to borrow them, and I wasn't supposed to have them in the house. But nobody had ever exactly told me not to read them.

"I'm not supposed to buy them," I argued. "And I didn't. I read Eddie and Dan's. And I wouldn't even have done that," I fibbed, "except Dan told me about Superman being classified 4-F, and I didn't believe him, and he said read it and see for yourself. And it was true. Superman tried to enlist and then flunked the eye test, just like you, Daddy."

My father poured himself more lemonade. I plunged on. "Because of his X-ray vision, Superman saw right through the wall and read the eye chart in the next room, which was different from the one in his room. So he got it all wrong. And he was 4-F. Superman!"

Daddy drank all his lemonade. Then he set down the glass and carefully wiped his mouth on his napkin. "I'll be darned, Ellen," he finally said, trying not to smile. "That is exactly what happened to me!"

1943

S I X

*M*y friends and I never got tired of the war. We saved newspapers and tin cans and bacon grease and hauled everything all the way to the collection center in Eddie's wagon. When the wagon broke, we found Marvin's old baby buggy down in his cellar and used it. We chewed as much Wrigley's Spearmint gum as we could and pooled our foil wrappers to make a tinfoil ball. Before we turned it in, we wanted it to be bigger than the one on display in the window of the Red Cross, and that one was as big as the globe in Miss Hennessy's classroom.

Miss Hennessy. She'd turned out to be just as bad as Miss Mackey as far as I was concerned. My parents didn't understand why I had so much trouble getting along with teachers. "Just do what they tell you and don't argue about everything" was my father's advice.

On my end-of-sixth-grade report card, Miss Hennessy wrote: "Ellen is bright and could do good work if she would settle down. But she jumps from one thing to the other and often does not finish what she starts. She participates in class discussions, but she does not like entertaining other points of view. Ellen needs to work on listening, following directions, and penmanship."

While my parents went over the report with me, my mind wandered. I couldn't help it. It happened all the time. My mind had a life of its own that seemed to have almost nothing to do with the rest of the world, and it took off and went where it wanted. This time, it got interested in "entertaining other points of view."

I would do it as a tap dancer—buck-and-wing! shuffle-off-to-Buffalo!—wearing shiny satin shorts and a red, white, and blue spangled blouse, with a top hat and a cane. It would be just like going overseas and entertaining the troops, which all the movie stars were doing. "Other points of view" in my imagination became a thousand clapping, whistling, cheering soldiers.

"Ellen," my father said, "are you listening?"

"She's smiling because she feels embarrassed. She knows she should be doing better in school," my mother put in, frowning at me and sending me eye signals. I wiped the smile off my face.

"Yes, Daddy," I said.

"Yes what?" he wanted to know.

I hesitated. I had no idea what he'd said to me. I'd been busy with my buck-and-wing, with my shuffle-off-to-Buffalo. "She understands," Mom said, "and next year she'll try harder."

My father was still frowning. "Ellen?" he said.

"I do," I assured him. "I will."

"About everything?" he asked.

"Everything," I promised.

"And you'll practice your handwriting over the summer?" I said I would. "All right, then," he said.

After he left the kitchen, Mom said, "Ellen, you shouldn't daydream when your father is talking to you. It's not respectful."

"I know," I said. "I'm sorry."

She sighed. "You're always sorry."

It was true. I always was sorry. But that didn't change anything. My mind went where it wanted to, and I had to go along.

Last fall, Dan had tacked up big maps of Europe and of Asia in his and Eddie's bedroom. The map of Europe was over his bed. The map of Asia was over Eddie's. Evenings, after he listened to the news, Dan stood on the beds in his stocking feet to mark the progress of the war in crayon, red for the enemy and blue for the Allies. You could tell how things were going just by glancing at the colored lines.

In the European part of the war, U.S. forces had joined the British in North Africa in November to fight against the Vichy French, the Germans, and the Italians.

I had hoped Uncle Bob would get sent to North Africa when he finished Communications School, so I took a special interest in what was going on there. I could find places in North Africa practically with my eyes closed. The Kasserine Pass. Casablanca. Oran. Fondouk. And in the encyclopedia, I read about the geography and the customs in that part of the world and found pictures of camels and donkeys pulling plows together, and of mosques and minarets.

It turned out to be a big waste of my time, because the letter we got from Uncle Bob when he finished his ten weeks of school said: "You'll never believe this, but I did so well I got assigned to the cadre, which means I am an instructor and will be staying here to teach. I got promoted, too, to Technician Third Grade, which is the same as corporal."

In spite of the promotion, I was very disappointed. "Uncle Bob's never going to see any action," I grumbled.

Mom was proud of Uncle Bob and glad to have him safe in Texas. "He must've been about the smartest one in his class," she bragged, "to be made an instructor."

Daddy seemed puzzled. "Bob was never much of a student before," he said. "I guess it's an honor."

"It may be an honor, but I think it's a big mistake," I told him. "How are we going to win this war if they don't send the best people right to the front, where they could do some good?"

"At first I felt frustrated about not going overseas," Uncle Bob's next letter said. "But you have to serve where they need you. And teaching is more interesting than I thought.

1943

"At night I sit at the PX with guys from just about every state in the forty-eight. They are swell people. Good buddies. We talk about everything."

"Bob was never a big talker before," my father remarked.

"If he was really in the war, he wouldn't have time for so much talking," I said.

"What's wrong with talking?" my mother wanted to know. "To listen to the two of you, you'd think talking was against the law."

The allies won in North Africa in May, and I was liberated from Miss Hennessy's class in June. Right about then we got this news from Uncle Bob: "I am just itching to see action, so I put in for reassignment to an Infantry division, and I got it! They will have to win the war in Texas and in the Pacific without Robert Parker, because I am on my way to Europe at last. By the way, I am a Technician Fourth Grade now. Same as a sergeant."

I imagined that after all the waiting, the Army would send Uncle Bob right straight into battle. But they didn't. His first letter from overseas came from England. "We are billeted in the west," he wrote, "in Hereford, out in the country. We are near a Royal Air Force (RAF) base. There is nothing to do when we are off duty except go to the pub in the village and play darts and drink warm beer. Warm beer is not because of the war. It is the way they drink it in England. Ugh!"

I stuck the letter in my pocket and went to Dan's after supper, to give him the news.

The summer evening sky was pure white, and the air was warm and still. I wondered how long Uncle Bob would be stuck in England, and I began to worry that the whole war would be over before Technician Fourth Grade Robert Parker got anywhere near the fighting.

"Uncle Bob's overseas," I told Dan.

"Time to put him on the map, then," he said. He led the way to his and Eddie's room. "Where'd they send him?"

"England," I told him with a sigh. "A place called Hereford, out in the country."

"England," said Dan. We kicked off our shoes and climbed up on his bed. Dan found Hereford and put a tiny green x there for Uncle Bob. He made the x carefully. Dan was proud of his maps, and he didn't want to mess them up. "Hereford," Dan said. "I sure hope he doesn't have to stay there for the rest of the war."

"Don't worry, he won't." I tried to sound confident. "Uncle Bob's not going to miss out on the fighting. He wouldn't let them do that to him."

Dan jumped up and down on his bed a couple of times. "Don't jump on the bed," his mother called from somewhere else in the house.

"How did she know?" I asked.

"She always knows," Dan said. "She has eyes and ears all over the place."

We put our shoes back on. "Uncle Bob won't let them keep him out of the action," I repeated as we headed outside to try to round up enough kids for a game of hide-and-seek.

Dan shrugged. "He's in the Army now," he reminded me. "He doesn't have a thing to say about what they do with him."

"Well, he requested reassignment and he got it, didn't he?"

"Yeah," Dan agreed reluctantly.

"He can just request reassignment again, then," I concluded. "Right?"

"I guess," Dan said.

"Well, he can," I insisted. "And he will. You'll see."

Marvin and Eddie were playing gin rummy behind the toolshed, and Lisa-Lotte was watching them. Nobody was interested in hide-and-seek. So I borrowed Eddie's mitt, and Dan and I went out and had a catch in his driveway until it was dark and the lightning bugs appeared.

Last year, we ran after them and caught them in jars to make lightning-bug lamps. We lined them up in a dark place and let the bugs fly around winking on and off inside the jars until they died. This year, we were content to sit and watch them flitting over the lawns, their greenish glowing stomachs blinking against the black background of the bushes.

Summer again. Warm evenings and close stars, lightning bugs, crickets clamoring half the night in the vacant lot next to my house. Uncle Bob in England, but much closer to the fighting than he'd been before. Summer again, and freedom. I really had nothing to complain about.

SEVEN

*W*e decided to start a summer club and fix up the toolshed to use as our clubhouse. We dragged some old bricks and warped boards out of Marvin's garage and made brick-and-board shelves across one side of the shed. Mom gave us a slightly mildewed rag rug she had stuck away. Then we each brought some stuff to share and put it on the shelves. We agreed that for the summer everything in the toolshed belonged to all of us, and we could use each other's things any time we wanted to.

We had checkers and Chinese checkers and dominoes and jacks and pickup sticks and two decks of cards, clothesline to use for jumping rope, and a coffee can full of marbles. We had an ancient softball and two dead tennis balls. We had a stack of comic books, a couple of Nancy Drew mysteries, and a copy of the Hardy Boys' *The Secret of the Caves*. Nobody was willing to leave bats or mitts or good baseballs in the shed. And I wouldn't share my roller skates.

We decided dogs and cats could come in, but no grownups and no other kids. Just Lisa-Lotte, Eddie, Marvin, Dan, and me. That was it. If we had other friends over to play, we couldn't bring them here. This clubhouse was private property. KEEP OUT Eddie wrote in huge blue chalk letters on the toolshed door.

"That'll just wash off when it rains," Dan told him.

"So what?" Eddie said gruffly.

Dan and Eddie were always ready to go at each other. They actually had a fight at lunch recess last spring. Just about every kid in school had stood and watched them roll around on the ground, punching each other's arms and backs and grunting and crying. Then Eddie bit Dan on the shoulder. And Dan howled. And Miss Mackey dragged them both to the principal's office.

Biting was low of Eddie, but it was the only way for him to win. He was madder than Dan, and much more of a fighter, but he's a shrimp and Dan is big for his age. I had a hard time deciding what I thought about Eddie not fighting fair. I knew it was wrong. But how else could he have won?

I thought Dan would kill Eddie, once they got off school grounds. If I'd been Eddie, I would have sought sanctuary in neutral territory, like escaped prisoners of war did. But all that happened was that they glared at each other and walked back and forth to school separately for the rest of the week.

"I thought Dan would get even with Eddie," I told

my mom. "I thought he would murder him once they got home."

"Brothers and sisters fight all the time," Mom said, not looking up from the shirt she was ironing. "But they don't stay mad."

"I would," I said. "I'd stay mad if someone bit me."

"That's 'cause you're an only child," Mom said.

That was my mother's answer to a lot of things, I'd noticed. I was "disputatious," she said, because I was an only child. I daydreamed and fibbed because I was an only child. I was a tomboy, I needed a lot of attention, I could entertain myself, I could carry on a sensible conversation with grownups, I was impatient, I was capable, I was stubborn, I was selfish. All because I was an only child.

"It's not my fault I'm an only child," I said. Mom didn't say anything. "Why am I an only child, anyway?"

Mom always gave me the same answer. She said, "Your father and I decided we could never love another child as much as we loved you, so we didn't have any more."

I hated this answer. Something about it made me feel sad.

My father's answer was better. "We couldn't afford more than you and your Uncle Bob," he said, "right smack in the middle of the Depression."

"Well, you could afford another one now," I suggested.

"At our age?" he said. "Don't be silly."

1943

Too bad. It would have been fun to have a baby brother or a sister. Especially with Uncle Bob away.

The first thing we decided to do, as a club, was to eat some early peaches and dry out the pits. Everyone would bring a nail file, and my father said he'd supply the sandpaper, since he had plenty at his shop, and by the end of the summer we'd have peach-pit rings.

"If you do," Mom told me, "you'll be the first. I don't know a single person who ever finished making a peach pit into a ring."

"I'll do it," I told her. "Wait and see."

"Mmmmm," she remarked.

The next thing we decided to do was plan an adventure hike. "Through the big drainpipes on the other side of the park," Eddie suggested.

"Over the abandoned railroad bridge," Marvin said.

"Through the streetcar tunnel," I added.

"I don't know," Dan said. "That's against the law."

"Yeah," said Marvin, "there's signs all over the place."

"I know," I said. "That's what makes it an 'adventure,' Marv." I crossed my eyes at him to show him what a cowardly baby I thought he was.

"What signs?" Lisa-Lotte wanted to know.

" 'No trespassing,' " Dan said.

" 'Railcars only,' " Eddie added.

" 'Private property, keep out!' " said Marvin.

Lisa-Lotte looked at me. "It sounds not possible."

"Of course it's possible," I said. "I've done it before."

"Oh, sure," said Dan.

I had. I'd done it with Eddie once. We had stepped into the curving tunnel and run next to the track from one end to the other before a streetcar came in either direction. We knew it was forbidden, and we swore we'd never tell anyone.

"I have!" I told Dan hotly.

Dan looked at his brother with narrowed eyes. Eddie examined a splinter on the bottom of one bare foot and picked at it with the nail file he'd brought to start smoothing out his peach pit.

"No streetcar tunnels," Dan said. "That's final. We don't want anyone to get run over."

"Well then, no drainage pipes," I said. "We don't want anyone to get caught in a flash flood and drown. And no railroad bridge—we don't want anyone to get dizzy and fall off. And no adventure hike, because you're a bunch of scaredy-cats."

"Shut up, Ellen," Eddie said, still digging at his foot.

"Yeah," said Marvin, reaching for a comic book off the top of the pile.

Dan and I glared at each other. "Okay," he said finally, "you win, Ellen. No adventure hike."

Our summer plans changed quickly. Before I knew what had happened, the boys were gone. They'd signed up to play baseball at the new recreation program over at the park.

1943

"Boys only," Eddie informed me. "Sorry, El."

"What do you mean, boys only?" I protested. "That's ridiculous." Eddie drew lines in the dust with one foot and didn't answer.

"What kind of a recreation program is this, anyway?" I demanded indignantly.

"A recreation program for boys," he said.

"I can play baseball as well as any boy!" I reminded him.

"Yeah. Well. That's not the point."

"I could cut off my hair," I suggested.

Eddie looked at me. He was thinking. A gnat hovered around the corner of his eye, and he brushed it away. "How short?" he asked.

"Short," I answered, "like a boy's. And you can lend me a pair of boy's jeans and one of your shirts. And call me Steve. Come on."

"Come on where?" he wanted to know.

"Come with me to get a scissors, so we can cut my hair."

"We?" he objected.

"Well, I can't cut the back of my own hair, can I?"

Eddie shuffled behind me, looking doubtful, all the way to my house and then all the way back to his. I got the chair from the toolshed and set it out in the yard. Then I sat down and handed Eddie the scissors.

"Ellen," he said, "I don't know how to do this."

"Just cut," I commanded.

"Okay," he said, "here goes."

Eddie breathed hard as he worked on my hair. The scissors I'd borrowed from Mom's sewing basket squeaked. I kept my eyes closed and sat as still as I could, listening to Eddie breathe, listening to the scissors squeak, and feeling hair fall on my eyelids and on my cheeks and down my neck.

Finally he stopped. "Finished?" I asked, brushing the hair off my face and opening my eyes.

Eddie stared at me unhappily. "I guess," he said.

"How do I look? Do I look like a boy?"

"I guess," he said, handing the scissors back to me.

"Great! I'll go check in the mirror, and you go get some of your clothes for me to wear." Eddie didn't move. "Okay?"

"Ellen," Eddie said, "this isn't going to work."

"Why not? What are you talking about? Do I look like a boy or don't I?"

"Well, you do and you don't. I mean, you do. But you still look like yourself. And lots of the kids will know you. And somebody will tell."

"You mean you chopped off my hair and then decided not to help me?" I asked. I couldn't believe that even Eddie would do something like that.

"I'm sorry, El," he said. "I thought you'd look all different without hair. But you don't. I'm really sorry."

The sneaky little coward turned and ran. I threw down the scissors and started to go after him, but I was distracted by how different my head felt when I moved, how I could feel the air around it in a way I never had before.

Just then Lisa-Lotte came around the corner of the toolshed. She took one look at me and lost her English. "*Mein Gott!*" she exclaimed.

1943

.　　.　　.

From then on, the boys were busy with baseball. And Lisa-Lotte usually had her nose in a book. What was I supposed to do all summer, sit around and wait for my hair to grow back?

"Maybe you could be on the radio," Mom suggested.

"Me?" I wondered, running my hand through the short hair on the top of my head, which felt a lot better than it looked.

"Maybe. I read about it in that paper they give away at the grocery. Station KFBB is doing programs for children. Plays, you know. On Saturdays. And they're auditioning kids to act in them."

My mother rummaged around in the pile of newspapers she was saving in the corner of the kitchen and found the page that told about the radio show.

"Here," she said, holding the paper up for me to see. "It says right here: 'Want to Be on the Radio? Child actors needed for Live Radio Plays. Call for information about auditions.' "

"What are auditions?" I asked.

"Trying out," she explained.

"What do you have to do to try out?" I asked.

"I don't know," my mother said.

Mom called up the radio station. All you had to do was come down there and read out loud. They would give you something to read when you got there.

"Easy as pie," Mom said. "And you're a good reader."

"I hate to read," I reminded her.

"You don't hate to recite. I remember last year . . ."

She put one hand over her heart and gazed into the distance. " 'By the shores of Gitche Gumee,' " she recited.

"Mom!"

" 'By the shining Big-Sea-Water . . .' "

"MOM!"

She was having fun. She swung her arm out, gesturing grandly. ". . . Stood the wigwam of Nokomis,/ Daughter of the Moon, Nokomis.' "

"It was an assignment," I protested. "I had to memorize it. I had to read it over and over so I could memorize it!"

"You didn't have to read it all day every day," she teased. "And what about, 'Listen, child, and you will hear . . .' " Mom frowned. "That's not right," she said.

" 'Listen, my children, and you shall hear / Of the midnight ride of Paul Revere,' " I coached.

"There! You see!" she said.

" 'On the eighteenth of April, in Seventy-five,' " I continued loudly," 'Hardly a man is now alive / Who remembers that famous day and year' "—I skipped to the end—" 'And the midnight message of Paul Revere'!"

"Enough!" Mom cried, joking, with her hands over her ears. "If we're going to get there in time for the audition, we have to get a move on."

"The audition is today?"

"This afternoon," she said. "I'm glad we called up right away. It's a good sign. We thought about it today, and it's happening today. That means we're supposed to do it. It probably means you'll get a part."

"But what about my hair?" I cried.

Mom hesitated. "What about it?" she asked.

"I can't go to an audition with my hair like this!"

I saw the flicker of agreement on my mother's face. But she caught herself. "Of course you can. You can go anyplace you need to go, hair or no hair. Besides, this is a radio audition. Nobody knows what you look like when they hear you on the radio. Come on!"

We raced upstairs to get ready. Mom put on a navy blue dress with tiny white flowers sprinkled all over it and a small white straw hat with a little veil that went across her forehead. She put her white purse and a pair of white gloves on the post at the top of the stairs and came into my room to see what was taking me so long.

I never really got dressed in the summertime. I wore shorts and T-shirts until school started, and then Mom took me downtown and bought me a pleated skirt or a kilt skirt with a big safety pin on the front and some white blouses to start school with. Later we'd go for snow boots and mittens and a new woolen hat and a muffler, if I'd lost the ones from the year before, which I always had.

Anyway, there I stood in my underwear looking into my closet when Mom bustled in, screwing on her pearl earrings as she walked.

"Not ready yet? We're going to be late!" She reached around me into my closet, pulled out a powder blue sundress, and dropped it over my head. Then

she handed me a pair of white ankle socks and my
sandals. She ran a hairbrush over my head a couple of
times and marched me into the bathroom, where she
swabbed my face and neck and elbows with a wet
washcloth. She pinched my cheeks hard and looked
me over.

"Let's go, Betty Grable," she said, calling me by
the name of one of her favorite movie stars.

If we'd had time, Mom would have put leg makeup
on her legs and I would have sat down on the floor and
drawn seams up the back of them with a black eyebrow pencil, so they'd look like stockings. But we
were in too much of a hurry.

The minute we got to the bus stop, the bus we
wanted wheezed up, and we hopped on. "See?" Mom
said, as I slid over to the open window and she sat
next to me. "Everything's going like clockwork. That
means good luck. Hair or no hair."

I gave my mother a look to let her know that I
thought her comment was unnecessary.

"Sorry," she said.

The radio station was in a shabby two-story building, nearly all the way downtown. It was stuffy and
hot inside, even though they had two electric fans
turned on in the windowless room where mothers and
kids were waiting.

Mom and I took the last two chairs. She smiled at
the roomful of people, picked up a magazine, and pretended to read. I looked around. The other mothers
were dressed up, too. They were powdered and per-

fumed. One of them was wearing stockings! I poked my mother to make sure she noticed. She sniffed. I knew she wished she had some, but she wouldn't buy anything on the black market. Not stockings. Not steak. Not sugar or butter or coffee or shoes. Not anything. And my father wouldn't, either. Anyway, my mother was the only one wearing a hat and pearl earrings, even though she didn't have stockings and hadn't had time to put makeup on her legs.

The boys looked pretty much like each other, the way they always did, in their striped T-shirts and dark pants.

The girls were another story. For one thing, they all had a lot of hair. One redhead had her curls piled on top of her head, and a blonde with a broad, serious face had braids wound around her ears. Another blonde had her hair hanging long and loose, and it went all the way to her waist. She had shining blue eyes and looked like the princesses in the storybooks they give you to read when you're little. The ones that remind you that you aren't anything like a princess.

The blue-eyed girl stared at me. I stared back.

"Don't stare," my mother whispered.

So I had to sneak looks at the princess, while she could just keep on staring straight at me. I felt the way a dog on a leash must feel when it meets a dog that's running around loose.

We all sat there for what seemed like a long time. Nobody said a word to anyone else. One very short boy whose feet came nowhere near to reaching the ground swung his legs back and forth, and the red-haired girl with the updo slouched in her chair with her arms crossed and a scowl on her face.

Finally the door to the studio opened and a man came out. He had a clipboard in his hand, his sleeves were rolled up, and his tie was loose. I could see sweat on his forehead.

"Come on in, kids," he said. He smiled over our heads at our mothers as we filed past him, and then he closed the door.

"Okay," he said, "this is the studio. That's the control booth, and the man you see inside the booth is the engineer. I'm the director."

As he spoke, he handed each of us some papers. "These are scripts," he explained. "And this is the microphone."

He adjusted the microphone down to the size of one of the smaller kids. "Now," he said, "there's nothing for you to be nervous about. What we want to do is hear how well you read—you know, expression and all —and hear how your voices sound over the mike. That's all there is to it. When it's your turn, you just step right up and read a few lines. If I push my hand up toward the ceiling, like this, it means louder. If I push my hand down toward the floor, it means softer. And if I push it toward you, it means step back, you're too close to the mike."

"What if we're not close enough?" one of the boys asked.

"I'll do the opposite," the director explained. "Okay? Everybody understand?"

The princess raised her hand. "Yes?" asked the director.

1943

"What are we trying out for?" she asked.

"Plays. To be broadcast on the radio. For children," answered the director.

"What I want to know is, what plays?" the princess asked.

"Oh, well, if you check your script, you'll see," he answered. "One is an old tale called 'Puss in Boots.' It's about a cat who outsmarts everyone."

We all looked at our scripts.

"And the other one is an original story, which I wrote myself, about the animals of the forest getting ready for winter. You know, collecting their food and saying goodbye to their little furry friends before they hibernate."

We all looked at him.

" 'Hibernate' means going to sleep for the winter," he said.

"We know that." I spoke up. "What animals?"

"Oh, a bear and a bunny and a squirrel and a chipmunk and all the cute little creatures in the forest," he answered. "Any more questions?"

There were none. He motioned to the bored-looking engineer. It was time to turn on the microphone and begin. The girl with the wound-around braids and a boy wearing a lanyard bracelet read first.

Everyone did a good job, I thought. We stumbled over a strange word here and there, and sometimes someone had to go back and begin again, to get the meaning right. But I thought everyone was good, and I wondered how the director would be able to choose.

After we had all read, some of us were called back to

read again. And then a few were called back a third time. The princess was. And I was, too.

The lines we read from "Puss in Boots" were funny and interesting. One time, after I read the part of Puss and the princess read the part of his master, the director said, "That was good. You two read well together."

The princess looked at me and smiled, as if to say, "Of course!" And I knew it really was my lucky day. I was going to play the bold, tricky cat and the princess was going to play my master, and we were going to get to know each other and be on the radio together. I couldn't wait.

Of course, we all had to read for the other play, too: the sappy little animals in the forest getting ready for winter. The smallest boy sounded a lot like a squirrel to me, and I thought he should get that part.

There were more kids piled up in the waiting room ready to audition after we finished. We went out, and they went in. And it was our turn to wait again.

Finally the director called everyone into the studio. We were practically standing on each other's feet. "These are tough decisions," he told us. "I need to go over my notes and talk with my engineer before I decide who will get parts. But I want to thank you all for coming down this afternoon. You've been terrific. Everyone did a fine job of reading—and of waiting. And I want to wish you luck. And to remind you, if you don't get a part, try not to be discouraged. It doesn't mean you're not a good actor. It just means there wasn't a part that was right for you."

He dismissed us. Someone would call next week to tell us the results of the audition.

On the way out, the princess touched my arm. "What's your name, Puss?" she asked in a friendly way. So she thought I'd get the cat's part, too!

"Ellen Parker," I answered.

"I'm Josephine Montgomery," she told me. "See you."

The week went slowly. My mother shooed me out of the house through the back door, and I came in the front. I couldn't stand to be away from the telephone. We got a few calls, but none for me.

When Mom went out, she'd say, "Take good care of the phone," teasing me. But when she came back, she'd ask, first thing, "Did they call?" She was as eager to hear the news as I was.

The director called up one afternoon while Mom was at the grocery store. I grabbed the phone on the first ring. "Congratulations, Ellen," he said. "You've gotten a part. I've chosen you for the lead in 'The Animals of the Forest.' You'll play the squirrel!"

"The squirrel?"

"The spunky squirrel who sets such a good example for the rest of his furry forest friends," said the director.

"The squirrel?"

"The squirrel," he said, "yes! The furry little guy who reminds everyone to get ready for the hard days ahead when they're so busy having fun in the summertime. You remember."

I did remember. And I was furious. I'd been count-
ing on playing the clever cat and on acting on the
radio with a girl who looked like a princess and
wanted to be friends with me. And now they were trying to give me the part of some stupid squirrel. Well,
somebody was going to have to play that part, but it
wasn't going to be me!

"I'm sorry," I said, making my voice very sweet
and very soft, the way I imagined Beth's voice
sounded in *Little Women*, when she was dying. "I'm
really sorry. But I can't take the part."

"You can't?"

"No. You see, we just found out I have polio," I
lied. "I'm in a wheelchair now, and we don't know
how to get it on the bus, so I can't come to the studio.
That's why I can't be the squirrel in your play."

"Polio!" he gasped. "Oh, I'm sorry!"

I hung up gently, the way I thought a very sick person would.

"Did they call?" Mom asked, as soon as she came
in.

I nodded yes.

"They called! What part did you get?"

I shook my head. I was all softness and sadness. "I
didn't get one," I told her. "He said he was sorry."

EIGHT

*L*isa-Lotte went to the local branch of the public library once a week. Usually I walked with her. We could go straight up our block and over about ten streets. That was an easy walk. Or we could follow the pathways through the vacant lots, starting with the one right next to my house, and risk getting grasshoppers in our socks, and stop to play on the rope swing hanging from an old oak tree, and make the walk longer and more interesting. Sometimes we did, and sometimes we didn't, depending on Lisa-Lotte's mood.

Once in a while, we went way out of our way to walk by the kiddie playground. Lisa-Lotte liked to sit near the wading pool and watch the babies splashing in the water. She was interested in babies. I wasn't. The only thing that interested me about babies was where they came from. And nobody had managed to give me what I considered a satisfactory answer about that.

"What do you mean," Lisa-Lotte asked, "where babies come from? You know where they come from. They come from their mothers"—she hesitated— "and their fathers."

I shrugged. "I guess," I said.

"You guess?"

"I mean, they do. Sure. But how?"

"How?"

"How do they get in?" I raised my voice. "How do they get out?"

"*Shhhh!*" Lisa-Lotte warned. She looked around us, but the tree-shaded sidewalks were deserted. On the blistering-hot summer afternoons, people closed up their houses and stayed inside. They did not run their errands when it was ninety degrees in the shade.

When we got to the library, Lisa-Lotte marched in through the tall, wide-open doors, and I waited on the steps outside, as usual.

I pulled out the peach pit I was working on, which I kept in my pocket with a piece of nearly worn-out sandpaper. It was the pit I'd gotten out of the first peach I ate, back in June. I'd been working on it ever since. Now the pit was perfectly smooth all over, and I was ready to start making the hole in the center of it, but I had no idea how. I didn't want to risk ruining it, so Lisa-Lotte was going to see if there was a book in the library that told how to make jewelry out of pits.

Lisa-Lotte took forever.

When she finally came out, she had several books.

"Did you get the one for me?" I asked, standing up and stuffing my peach pit and the sandpaper back into my pocket.

Lisa-Lotte nodded.

"Neat-o!" I said. "Let's see."

"Not here," she said. "When we are home. You must wait."

Lisa-Lotte could be stubborn. She was holding the books behind her and backing toward the sidewalk.

I shrugged. "Okay," I said. I didn't feel like arguing. After all, she had the book. I could wait until I got home to find out how to finish my ring.

Lisa-Lotte carried the books, and I walked next to her, doing a front walkover from time to time, just to make the trip less boring. When we got home, I asked her for the book.

"I will tell my mother I am back," she said. "And then I will tell her you and I are to look together at books for a while."

Lisa-Lotte's mother wasn't as strict as she had been at first. She worried more about Lisa-Lotte than anyone else's mother worried about anything. But she let her come to my house. And she let her go to Eddie's and Marvin's, too, if their mom was home. Slowly, she seemed to be getting used to her new life in America.

"I just want to look at the one book," I reminded Lisa-Lotte as she disappeared down her steps.

When she came over a little while later, she had one book tucked under her arm. We went up to my room, and she put her finger to her lips and quietly closed the door. Then she handed me the book. It was called *Human Reproduction.*

I handed it back to her. "You brought the wrong book."

Lisa-Lotte gave it back to me. "This book is not wrong."

"What about the book I wanted? The one about making rings out of peach pits?"

"Oh, they have no such book," she told me. "I asked the librarian. But I thought this one would interest you, too. Does it not?"

"Not if it just tells the same old thing," I said. "Because I don't believe a word of it."

Lisa-Lotte sat down on my bed, and I sat next to her. She opened the book. "Let me look," I said, taking it from her and flipping to the end, where the information, if there was any, was bound to be. I looked at a couple of pages and tossed it aside. I was disappointed about not getting the book I needed. And now this.

Lisa-Lotte looked at me. "What can be the matter?" she asked. "You said you wanted to know about babies, how they get in and how they get out. Here is a book from the adult section of the library that tells us just those things."

She took back the book. I lay down with my hands clasped behind my neck and looked out my window at the leaves of a big sycamore tree. They were covered with fine, white August dust, dust from the parched fields and the dried-up creeks, dust that was as much a part of the last month of summer as the stifling heat and the cloudless sky.

"That book says exactly what Eddie told me two years ago," I said. "I didn't believe him then and I don't believe it now." I looked crossly at Lisa-Lotte. "You can't believe everything you read in a book, you know."

"But, Ellen, this is the way!" she insisted. "This is the way they get in. This is the way they get out. Even my mother has told me so!"

I stared out the window. My mother had told me, too. And Eddie had. And here was this book, full of drawings of sperms and eggs and babies growing. But I still felt the whole thing was ridiculous.

"Ellen," Lisa-Lotte protested, "how can you say you do not believe it when this is the way it is? You have to believe it."

I stared at the leaves. Not one of them moved. There wasn't a breath of air outside. It was blazing hot. And my room, with the door closed, was beginning to feel like the inside of an oven. I swung my legs over the side of my bed and stood up. "Everybody doesn't have to believe the same things, Lisa-Lotte," I told her firmly. "America is a free country. We can believe what we want to."

Lisa-Lotte started to argue, but changed her mind. She took the book home and then came back out and joined me, sitting on the curb in front of Eddie's and waiting for the ice cream man.

While we waited, I reached into my pocket for my sandpaper and my peach pit. The sandpaper was there. But the pit wasn't. I stood up and fished around in the bottom of one pocket, and then I tried the other. No pit. It must have fallen out on the way home, when I did one of those walkovers.

I sat back down next to Lisa-Lotte. "I lost my peach pit," I told her, running my hands through my short hair.

Lisa-Lotte looked upset. "We should search," she said. "We should go back right now and see if we can find her. It."

I thought about that. Walking all the way back to the library in the heat. Missing the ice cream man. And even if I found it, still not knowing how to make my peach pit into a ring.

"I don't think we'd find it," I said. "Anyway, it doesn't matter." We were both quiet. Then I said, "Maybe there's no such thing as a peach-pit ring. Maybe that's why nobody knows how to finish making one. Maybe peach-pit rings are just something everyone *wants* to believe in," I said, putting my chin in my hands, "like that stuff about babies."

NINE

*U*ncle Bob wrote to us often from England. "My buddy came up with two bicycles, one for him and one for me," he wrote. "We ride them down to the pub. It is a pretty ride through the countryside. There are larks in the bushes, and when they fly, they fly straight up in the air. I have never seen a bird do that before.

"We met some RAF pilots at the pub. They were only about twenty-three years old, but they were finished flying. They had been on so many missions they were worn out and couldn't fly anymore.

"That's the way it is. After so many years of war, people in England are just worn out. So it's a good thing us Yanks are here."

When I wrote back to Uncle Bob, I used a thin sheet of paper that folded over and made itself into its own envelope.

My Wartime Summers

I sat at the kitchen table for a long time, trying to decide what to say. Finally I wrote: "Dear Uncle Bob, How are you? I am fine. Marvin's cat had kittens, but the father cat killed them. We buried them in Marvin's back yard. Dan put a green x on his war map of Europe to show where you are. When you go someplace else, he will put another x and draw a line between them. Daddy says the biggest city in England is London. Do you ever go there? Where did your buddy get the bikes? I would like to have a bike. But we can't buy one until they start making them again after the war. Dan is the only kid on the block who has a bike. And you know Dan. He won't share it. Love, Ellen."

Uncle Bob wrote back: "Dear Ellen, I was very happy to get a letter from you. I can't tell where my buddy got the bikes. I promised. Any time I get a pass, I take the train to London. There is a big Red Cross canteen in Leicester Square (when you say it, you say Lester) where GIs go. During the Blitz, Londoners slept in the underground subway stations, which make good bomb shelters. A lot of the children have been sent to live in the country for safety, even though their parents can't go with them. When I come home I'll teach you how to ride Dan's bike if you don't have one yet. If he says no, I'll give him a knuckle sandwich.

"My buddies and I are ready to fight. We want to see some action. But I guess that won't happen until—" The next part of Uncle Bob's letter had been stamped over in black ink.

I showed my father the letter. "Censored," he told me. "They must've thought Bob was giving too many details. That's what the censor is for, to check the letters and make sure nobody tells anything that would endanger the troops."

I couldn't imagine Uncle Bob doing a dumb thing like that. And I didn't like it that someone had read a letter he wrote to me and cut something out.

"There's a war on," my father reminded me when I complained.

"What about the Four Freedoms?" I wanted to know. We had memorized them at school last spring.

"What about them?"

"Freedom of speech and expression," I said, "that's the first freedom. If someone is cutting stuff out of Uncle Bob's letters, he doesn't have freedom of expression."

"True," my dad said. "But . . ."

"I know, 'there's a war on,' " I fumed. "And here I thought that was what the war was all about!"

My dad looked puzzled.

"About freedom," I reminded him. "I mean, isn't that what we're fighting for?"

"Sure it is," he said. "But you can't be in the armed forces and have freedom. How could you win a war that way?"

At the bottom of Uncle Bob's letter was a row of O's and X's. Hugs and kisses. "At least the censor didn't cut out my hugs and kisses," I said.

"Dear Uncle Bob," I wrote, "They are reading your letters to me and cutting parts out. I thought you ought to know. I do not think it's right that soldiers do not have freedom of expression, which is one of the Four Freedoms. Love, Ellen, XXXXXXXXXXXXXXOOOOOOOOOOOOOO"

"Dear Ellen," Uncle Bob answered, "Soldiers have two of the Four Freedoms. They have freedom of religion and they have freedom from want. But they do not have freedom of expression. And they do not have freedom from fear. Love, Uncle Bob, XXXOOO"

1944

TEN

*T*he first we heard about the invasion was on the evening news: "... Under the command of General Eisenhower, Allied naval forces, supported by air forces, began landing Allied armies on the northern coast of France."

"Bingo! There goes Bobby!" my excited father cried.

"Are you sure?" my mother asked, her voice small with worry. "Would a radio operator have to be part of this?"

"They couldn't have an invasion without communications units," my father explained. "The guys with the radios, they have to be up where the fighting is. Right smack up at the front."

It was Tuesday, June 6, 1944. School was out, Miss Jennings and I would never have to tangle again, and the invasion of Europe had finally begun.

Early the next morning, I went over to Dan and Eddie's. I hadn't been to their house in months. We didn't tramp back and forth the way we used to. My mother said, "Thank goodness! I got pretty tired of wiping Eddie's fingerprints off my clean white refrigerator." But I could tell she missed him, just the same.

Dan and Eddie were in their kitchen, eating breakfast. Eddie wasn't even dressed. He was in his pajama bottoms, reading the contest rules on the back of the cornflakes box and feeding himself without looking. Dan was studying the morning newspaper and listening to the radio at the same time. I rattled the screen door so they'd know I was there. Then I let myself in.

"D-Day!" was Dan's triumphant greeting.

It had been about a year since I'd bothered with Dan's maps. I didn't need them. I could follow the war perfectly well now by looking at the maps in the papers. But on the morning that more than 150,000 American, British, and Canadian troops finally landed in France, I wanted to see it laid out on Dan's bedroom wall. And I wanted to watch Dan make another careful x for Uncle Bob on the coast of France and draw a green line between the x in England and the new one.

"I told you the Allies would invade through France," Dan said.

"I never said they wouldn't," I countered.

"You did," he reminded me. "Last spring, you said Italy, remember?"

"I said Italy or France, one or the other," I bluffed. "That's what I remember."

"Well, I always knew it would be France," he bragged.

"So did I," Eddie said.

"Don't talk with your mouth full," Dan told him.

"We need to move Uncle Bob," I said.

"Are you sure?" Dan asked.

"Of course I am."

"How can you be sure he's part of the invasion?"

"Come on, Dan, what do you think he's been doing in England all this time?"

"What?" asked Eddie, through a mouthful of cereal.

"Getting ready to invade, of course," I answered.

"Are you positive?"

"Of course I am. What else would he have been doing?"

Eddie shrugged and went back to reading.

"There are plenty of other things," Dan said.

"I guess," I admitted. "But last night, when we heard, my father said, 'There goes Bobby.' "

Dan thought that over. Then he nodded. "Probably," he agreed. But he wouldn't make another green x until I was certain. Crayon was impossible to erase, and he had to be careful about messing up his map. Nothing I could say would persuade him to move Uncle Bob until I had the name of someplace to move him to.

Dan showed me the coast where the landing was taking place. "They could land on any one of these beaches," he explained, "or on all of them. I can't move him until we know."

"Okay," I said reluctantly, squinting at the coast of

France, imagining that if I looked hard enough, I
might be able to see the actual invasion taking place,
the way I could see whole armies of knights and
horses doing battle if I squinted long enough at the
marbly linoleum in our kitchen. "Okay, I'll wait. But
the minute I know where he is, you have to move
him." I had the feeling it would be bad luck not to.
Dan's maps seemed important again.

"I'll move him," Dan promised, walking back to
the kitchen with me, "as soon as you can tell me
where he is."

I pushed open the screen door. " 'Bye, El," Eddie
said, with his mouth full.

The rest of June passed, but we didn't hear from
Uncle Bob.

At the movies we saw the Paramount News report
about D-Day. We saw the big ships unloading amphibians crammed with American soldiers wearing
helmets and heavy packs and carrying weapons and
equipment. And we saw the soldiers running down
the ramps right into the rough water and then trying
to wade ashore.

The ones who made it to the beach snaked forward
frantically on their elbows. The ones who didn't lay
facedown while bullets from the German guns posi-
tioned on the cliffs above pocked the water all around
them and the next wave of soldiers struggled past.

Some people said if the amphibians had come in
closer before they unloaded, there would have been
fewer casualties. I asked my father why they didn't.

"Well," he replied, "conditions at the beaches where the Americans landed were bad. High waves and all. Kept them back. And some of the crews just wanted to get their landing craft out of the danger zone."

"You mean they didn't come in closer, because they were scared?" My father nodded. "But that wasn't fair!" I exclaimed.

"Things like that happen in the heat of battle, Ellen," my father said.

I didn't want to believe this. I decided my father's first explanation was right. The water was rougher than the amphibian crews expected. They couldn't get any closer to the beaches than they did.

In spite of the thousands of casualties, the invasion was a success, because now the Allied liberation of Europe was under way.

We were thrilled to think that the end of the war was in sight and that we were going to win it. All we had to do now was march through France and Belgium and Holland to Germany, invade Germany and get rid of Hitler, and it would be over. Except for the Japanese, of course.

"If Bob was killed or wounded," my father said, trying to comfort my mother, "we'd have heard by now."

"But how can you be sure?" Mom asked. She had the awful feeling that something bad had happened to Uncle Bob.

"I can be sure because common sense tells me that

the U.S. Army is not going to be able to send polite notes to people letting them know that their relatives are safe. It's only going to be able to send bad news," Dad replied.

I made a fake telegram for my mother and left it at her place at the table. "TECHNICIAN FOURTH GRADE ROBERT PARKER IS ALIVE AND WELL SOMEWHERE IN FRANCE STOP," my telegram said. "HE GOT WET LANDING ON OMAHA BEACH STOP HE GOT SAND UP HIS NOSE STOP BUT THINGS ARE A-OK NOW STOP AND HE IS PROCEEDING TO INVADE EUROPE STOP HE IS TRADING CANDY BARS FOR FRESH EGGS STOP HE IS WELCOMED BY THE PEOPLE STOP"

The fake telegram made my mother smile. But we still didn't hear anything real about Uncle Bob, and as far as she was concerned, every day we didn't hear from him gave us more to worry about.

Dad stubbornly disagreed. "No news is good news," he insisted.

I agreed with both of them. I was dying to find out where Uncle Bob was now. And I was afraid to hear that something bad had happened to him, too. Bad things were happening to a lot of people.

A house right up at the end of the next block had a gold star hanging in the living-room window. A gold star, to show that someone in the family had been killed in the war. And over near the library, Lisa-Lotte and I saw a window with two gold stars in it, hanging side by side.

"No news is good news." I repeated what my father said to Dan and Eddie and anyone else who asked me if we'd heard from Uncle Bob. Even Mrs. Anger, who asked with that sly face, just hoping for bad news about anything. "No news is good news, Mrs. Anger," I told her, making my voice cheerful and polite so she'd have nothing to complain about.

"I guess no news is good news," Eddie said, sounding disappointed, as if he might just want to hear any kind of news.

"Don't forget to let me know," Dan said impatiently, eager now to follow Uncle Bob all the way to Germany, green x after green x, connected with a neat green line—like one of those join-the-dot pictures we used to like to do when we were little.

"As soon as I hear," I told him. "The minute."

I couldn't help wondering how it would be if what I heard was bad, if what I heard was that Uncle Bob had been hit first thing, wading in toward the shore, holding the radio—which my father had told me was a damn heavy piece of equipment—high up over his head. What if he was one of the ones we'd seen, pitched over facedown in the water?

When I caught myself thinking things like that, I spoke to myself sternly, as if I were my father. "No news is good news," I told myself. "There's no point in worrying about something you can't do anything about."

Something else that happened that nobody could do anything about and that worrying didn't help had happened in the spring, before the invasion. What happened was, Lisa-Lotte got breasts.

"Can you still see your feet when you look down?" I wanted to know. Lisa-Lotte wouldn't answer, so I asked my mother.

Mom made a face. "Now, what do you think?" she said. I shrugged. I didn't know. That's why I was asking.

Right before school was out for the summer, one of the boys in the eighth grade, the class ahead of us, sneaked up behind Lisa-Lotte and snapped the elastic in the back of her bra. Then he ran off with a couple of his stupid friends, all of them snorting and punching one another.

"Do you want me to beat him up for you?" I offered.

Lisa-Lotte shook her head no and looked at the ground. Her cheeks were bright red and there were tears in her eyes.

"I will if you want me to," I offered again. But she said no. I was relieved. The eighth-grade boys in our school seemed rough and wild all of a sudden. And some of them had gotten really big. I wasn't exactly afraid of them, but I wasn't so sure I could beat them up anymore, either. Though I might have to try it, if one of them snapped the back of my bra someday.

Happily, that wasn't a problem I was going to have very soon, if ever. I didn't have breasts. And I'd overheard my mother talking about it on the phone with her cousin. "Flat as a board," she said. "Takes after you, Vicky."

Flat-as-a-board was fine with me. I wasn't in any hurry to wear a bra, which Lisa-Lotte said was torture. And I didn't look forward to having to fight with boys for sneaking up behind me and being obnoxious.

The letter we'd been waiting for finally came—from England! Uncle Bob had missed the invasion. He'd been in the hospital with appendicitis, he wrote, and they'd had the party without him.

"See?" Dad said to Mom. "And you were so sure something had happened to him."

"Something did happen to him," I pointed out. "He had appendicitis."

The next letter we got came from London. "Here I am," he wrote, "still waiting. I wish I could have stormed those beaches with my buddies.

"The Germans are sending rockets over. They're like small, pilotless planes. We call them doodlebugs. They make a motorcycle sound up in the air. As long as you can hear them, you are okay. But when the noise stops, it means they are about to explode. Then you hit the pavement and hold your breath.

"The buzz bombs remind people here of the Blitz back in 1940 when the Germans tried to bomb England into surrendering. Even though they managed to hold out, the English people suffered a lot. So this new attack makes them feel discouraged, in spite of the invasion."

There was a snapshot with the letter: Uncle Bob and another soldier and a bike and a girl. The other soldier was holding the bike, and Uncle Bob had his arm around the girl. Uncle Bob and his buddy had on uniforms, but no hats or ties. And the girl was wearing a coat that looked too small for her. Uncle Bob and his buddy were both smiling at the camera. The girl was looking at Uncle Bob, and her face was lost in a shadow. On the back, Uncle Bob had written: "My buddy Mike and me and Edna, April 1944. Hereford."

"Would you look at that," my mother said. "Bob's the one with the girl!"

"He seems okay," my father said, studying the photograph and then handing it to me.

I stared hard at Uncle Bob, who looked very different from the way I remembered him. I wasn't sure if I met him walking down the street that I'd know who he was. My mother seemed to read my mind. "I wonder if the two of you will recognize each other by the time he gets home," she said thoughtfully, "both of you changing so much."

"I don't know what you're talking about," I lied, handing the picture back. "He's just the same, and so am I. When Uncle Bob gets home, everything is going to be exactly the way it was, and nobody is going to have trouble recognizing each other."

My parents exchanged a look, which of course I saw, but they didn't argue with me.

I went over to Dan's the next day. "Uncle Bob's in London," I reported.

"You want me to move him to London?" Dan asked, sounding annoyed.

"You said," I reminded him. He sighed and led the way to his bedroom. I sat down on Eddie's bed, and Dan kicked off his shoes and stood on his. He made a tiny green x at London and connected it with a very short line to the x at Hereford.

"Uncle Bob says he hopes he gets to France before the party's over," I told Dan.

"He better hurry," Dan said. "It'll be over in another month. It's practically over now. Hitler's done for."

I decided I wouldn't mind so much, having the war in Europe end and having Uncle Bob come home.

"Uncle Bob wants to get back to his own unit," I told Dan. "He wants to be back with his buddies."

"If there's any of them left," Dan said.

"Why wouldn't there be?"

"Depends which beach they came in on," he said. "They might've all been killed on the beach, if it was Omaha."

Sometimes Dan got carried away. "If all Bob's buddies got killed on the beach, this war would be in a fine fix," I reminded him, "without any radio communication."

Dan looked at me with pity. "Do you really think the whole war in Europe, the whole invasion of Europe, is depending on *one* communications unit?" he asked.

"They didn't all get killed," I muttered, embarrassed by my mistake.

ELEVEN

*I*t had been pouring down rain all day. My mother and Mrs. Siegel were having coffee at the kitchen table. They were friends now, and often spent time together. My mother got the whole story from Mrs. Siegel. How Mr. Siegel's store and a lot of other stores owned by Jews were destroyed by Nazis back in the 1930s, when Hitler was just getting started. How the Siegels managed to get out of Germany in 1939 on the very last boat that was allowed to unload German refugees in the United States. And how all their furniture and clothing and family pictures and dishes and silverware and books were on the next boat, which was turned back from New York Harbor, as the Siegels and others stood waiting on the dock. How they had lived for several years with relatives in New York City before Mr. Siegel's second cousin gave him a job and they moved out here.

Mrs. Siegel still longed for her other life, and for her furniture, too. You could tell. But she wasn't as frightened now. And with my mother to be friends with, she wasn't as lonely, either.

Mrs. Siegel was crocheting, Mom was darning socks, and Lisa-Lotte, who had decided she was going to be a dress designer, was sitting at the table with them, drawing clothes. I was up on the kitchen counter watching raindrops race each other down the window over the sink. I was making bets on them in my head. Money bets. So far I was just breaking even, but I still hoped to make a killing.

If I had a puppy, which I desperately wanted, I would have been playing with it, instead of racing raindrops. But I didn't have one, and my parents both said I had to put it out of my mind until after the war. They couldn't feed a dog with a clear conscience, they said, when people all over the world were starving.

I could not understand what one thing had to do with another, and I told them so. It was the same as the way they made me eat every last scrap of food on my plate, "because of the starving children in Europe." As if eating stuff I didn't have room for was going to make a single starving child less hungry.

"There is no connection between what I eat and the children who are starving," I reasoned. But my parents were united, and the subject was closed.

"Well, this'll probably be the last long summer for

these girls," my mother said to Mrs. Siegel. "They're getting old enough to think about summer jobs, I'd say."

Mrs. Siegel looked alarmed and puzzled. "To have jobs, before they are finished becoming their education?" she asked.

"Oh, I don't mean full-time ones," my mother said. "I mean in the summer, when there's no school, they can't just keep hanging around like this. They're getting too big."

"I have never had one job," Mrs. Siegel said, still having trouble with the idea.

"I did," my mom said happily. "When I was their age, I was already making money baby-sitting, and when I was in high school, I helped out my aunt on Saturdays. She was a milliner."

"So?" asked Mrs. Siegel.

"Milliner," my mother explained, "made hats for ladies."

"So." Mrs. Siegel nodded.

"And I gave piano lessons to all the kids in the neighborhood," my mother continued. "I did that after school and in the summers, too. And I had so much saved up, when Frank gave me my engagement ring I had enough to take the train to Chicago and buy myself a trousseau at Marshall Field's. I never will forget that, I can tell you. And then I had enough left over to pay for the food at the wedding, besides. And the whole time, I had to go against my parents to do it. My parents didn't like the piano lessons one bit. They were afraid I'd end up a spinster, like old Miss

Reeves, who taught me to play piano in the first place." She laughed, as if to say, "Me, a spinster—what a foolish thing for them to worry about!"

"Spinster?" inquired Mrs. Siegel, smiling back at Mom.

"An unmarried woman," my mother explained.

"Oh," said Mrs. Siegel, nodding.

"Why, I was the first one married, right out of high school. The very first one of all my friends. They should have known better than to worry about me."

Lisa-Lotte looked up. "You could teach piano lessons now," she said.

"No, I couldn't, hon," my mother told her. "For one thing, Mr. Parker wouldn't allow it. And for another, I don't have a piano!" She laughed, as if this were a joke. But I remembered once she told me how hurt she was when her mother died and left the piano to her aunt instead of to her.

"I might decide to be a spinster," I said, watching three raindrops reach the bottom of the window in a dead heat.

There was a pause. "Yes," my mother said thoughtfully, "I guess you might."

Then she got up and cleared the coffee cups and the plate of Fig Newtons off the table, poking me to move out of her way so she could put the dishes in the sink.

"Look there," she said, peering out the window over my shoulder, "there's a moving van parked at the end of the block! Ellen, why didn't you say something?"

"I didn't see it."

"Didn't see it? You've been looking out that window for an hour!"

"I haven't been," I said. "I've been racing raindrops."

"Lord," my exasperated mother said, "you are the original can't-see-the-forest-for-the-trees!"

I wasn't sure she'd said what she meant, but I got the point. And she was right. I'd been so focused on the raindrops, I hadn't noticed the moving van, the first one on our block since the housing shortage started, way back at the beginning of the war.

The movers were parked in front of the six-family apartment building at the far end of our street, and the moving men had already lowered a ramp and started to unload.

"Let's go watch, Lisa-Lotte," I said, jumping down.

"But it rains!" her mother objected.

"Not so much anymore," Mom said. "Here." She handed each of us a piece of newspaper to hold over our heads and hustled us out the door. "Walk in between the raindrops so you don't melt!" she called after us.

I knew my mother would have liked to come with us and try to find out how the new neighbors had managed to get the apartment and see exactly what the movers were taking into their place. But she couldn't. Only kids could do stuff like that.

Luckily, the rain stopped almost the minute we got outside, and the clouds just rolled on by, the way they will in summer. The air was thick and warm, and the

sun came out, and before long you could see mist ris-
ing from the pavement. Lisa-Lotte and I sat on our
newspapers across the street on Marvin's front steps,
the closest we could get without being in the way.

After the movers had carried in a dining-room set
and a huge red-and-green Chinese dragon lamp and a
four-poster bed and a pale green love seat, a station
wagon pulled up in front of the van. A woman who
looked like the movie star Rosalind Russell jumped
out of the driver's side and a girl about our age got out
of the passenger seat.

They stood with their arms around each other and
watched the movers carry in their stuff. Every once in
a while, the woman would call, "Watch that!" or
"Take it easy, there!" in a friendly way, and the movers would be extra careful carrying the vanity table
with the skirt or the big mirror with the gilt edges or
the chandelier with the crystal teardrops hanging
down. At the end, the movers took in a Victrola and
two big boxes marked RECORDS.

When the truck pulled away, Lisa-Lotte and I were
still sitting there. "Hey!" the woman called to us,
waving as she went into the building.

The girl didn't say anything, but she looked at us
carefully before she turned and followed her mother.
She looked at us, and we looked at her. She was just
like her mother, beautiful, with dark hair pinned back
and pale skin, with a straight, short nose and a wide
mouth. And breasts.

TWELVE

*T*he next afternoon, my mother sent me over to the new neighbors' with a tuna casserole. "Are you sure?" I asked, holding the casserole in both hands and hesitating by our door.

"Sure I'm sure," she told me. "It's what you do for new people. Send over something for them to eat so they don't have to worry about cooking while they're getting unpacked."

I set off with the casserole.

In the boiling-hot middle of the summer afternoon, the street was completely deserted. Out of the corner of my eye, I caught the slight movement of Mrs. Anger's curtain. Otherwise, there wasn't a living thing in sight. Except me, in my faded shorts and T-shirt, with my hair in two short, skinny braids, carrying a tuna-fish casserole.

1944

A new-looking label on one of the mailboxes said DARLING, DARLENE AND CLARE. Which was Darlene, I wondered, as I pushed hard on the bell underneath their names, and which was Clare?

I could hear music coming from the first-floor apartment in the back. The Glenn Miller band. I waited until the record stopped, and rang again. But when I heard the Andrews Sisters start, I just followed the sound of the music and banged on the door with the toe of my shoe. Somebody lifted the needle off the record carelessly, so it made a scratching sound.

I waited, holding the casserole out in front of me. When the door opened, it was the girl. She was wearing a white towel wound around her head like a turban, white shorts, and a white halter top. Her feet were bare, and her straight brown toes had red-painted nails.

Inside my shoes, I curled my skinny toes under in embarrassment.

"My mother sent this," I said. "Tuna and noodle."

She looked steadily at me, with turquoise eyes—turquoise eyes! "Want to come in?" she asked.

"Okay," I said, thrusting the casserole at her. "Here." She took the dish and set it down on top of the nearest packing box.

"It needs to go in the refrigerator," I told her.

"Okay," she said. But she didn't move the dish.

"I'm Ellen Parker. I live down at the other end of the block in the brown house next to the vacant lot."

"I'm Clare," she said. "I live—here!" She did a neat

turn and gestured grandly at the mess. Then she flopped down on the pale green love seat I'd seen the movers carry in, and folded her arms. "We haven't hardly started to unpack," she complained. "My mother went to work, and she left it all for me to do." She giggled. "But I haven't done a thing except my own room. Want to see?"

I followed her to the back of the apartment, where she had managed to make up her four-poster bed with white flounces and to put the canopy on all by herself. Her stuffed animals were piled in the center of the bed, and the big oval mirror with the gilt frame stood grandly in one corner of the room. Her collection of tiny glass animals was on the top of the dresser, right next to a silver brush and comb set and six different colors of nail polish in slender bottles.

"Looks like you got a lot done," I observed.

"I guess," Clare said. "But what I was supposed to do was unpack the stuff in the kitchen."

"We could do it now," I offered. "It wouldn't take two of us very long."

"My mother wants all those shelves lined before I unpack one thing," she said.

On the way to the kitchen, I picked up the tuna casserole and then stuck it in the empty refrigerator.

Clare and I worked for the rest of the afternoon, lining the kitchen shelves and drawers with brand-new blue-and-white-patterned oilcloth and unpacking the dishes and the pots and pans and utensils and putting them away.

It was hot work. We opened the back door and the

kitchen window and put a small fan on top of the refrigerator. But even so, I could feel the sweat running
down my back, and pretty soon the waistband on my
shorts was soaked and dark. Clare had tiny beads of
perspiration on her upper lip.

"Some people sweat a lot more than others do," I
said.

"Mmmm," said Clare, handing me a stack of flowered china dishes to go up on the topmost shelf. "We
hardly ever use these," she explained.

Clare's father, it turned out, had moved to Los Angeles, California. He was not in the movie business, as
I hoped when she told me. But he did own a grocery
store. "And he's buying up beachfront property,"
Clare said, "just as fast as he can."

"What's 'beachfront'?" I asked.

"On the beach," she answered, an impatient edge
in her voice. "Next to the ocean."

Clare's father and Darlene (she called her mother
Darlene) were thinking about a divorce. But for now,
it was just a separation.

"Darlene cried a lot at first," Clare told me. "But I
think she's getting used to it."

"Are you getting used to it?" I asked.

"Sort of," Clare answered.

"A lot of people don't have fathers around," I said,
jumping down from the counter where I'd been standing to put the dishes up on the top shelf. "I mean,
with so many of the fathers in the war. You could pretend your father was in the Army if you wanted to.
Then you wouldn't have to feel bad."

Clare giggled. "My father is fifty years old," she said. "It's pretty hard to imagine him in a uniform!"

"My uncle's in the Army," I boasted. "He's still in England, but he's going to France any minute, to be part of the invasion. He doesn't want to miss the party."

"What party?" Clare asked.

"The invasion of Europe," I explained, "the last bit of the war. Walking to Germany and knocking on Hitler's door."

"I didn't think it was going to be that easy," Clare said.

"It's going to be pretty easy," I assured her. "The Germans are on the run. They know they've lost. It will all be over by Christmas."

Clare shrugged. "If you say so," she said.

Darlene was a receptionist in a doctor's office. The next day was her day off. They were going to the pool, Clare said. I could come with them if I wanted to. Before we knew it, she reminded me, it would be August, the polio month, when nobody dared to go swimming or to the movies, either. When your parents insisted that you stay away from crowds.

"I'll ask," I said. Clare raised an eyebrow.

A snowstorm paperweight was on top of one of the boxes. I picked it up and shook it, and watched as the snow swirled around the snowman, who stood forever at the center of the storm.

"It's rude to touch things," Clare said, taking the paperweight out of my hand.

"When I've been touching your stuff all afternoon?" I said.

1944

Clare opened the door. I stood there for a moment, undecided. Then, "What about Lisa-Lotte?" I asked. "Can she come swimming with us?"

Clare said, "Who's she?"

"Lisa-Lotte Siegel, my best friend. She was with me yesterday."

"Oh, yeah," Clare remembered. "I guess," she said.

"Good," I said. "I'll tell her." I stepped out the door. It seemed that Clare was in a hurry to close it now. Her mind was suddenly on something else. "See you tomorrow," I said.

Clare shut the door.

I called Lisa-Lotte when I got home. At first she said she didn't want to go. Then she said she didn't think her mother would let her go. Then she said she was sure her bathing suit didn't fit her anymore. The last thing was true. My mother volunteered to lend Lisa-Lotte hers. It was a one-piece yellow suit with skinny straps and a skirt. Lisa-Lotte came over to try it on.

"It's perfect on you, Lisa-Lotte," Mom told her. "It's a lot prettier on you than it is on me. And I never go to the pool anyway. Why don't you just keep it?" My mother was nice that way.

At noon the next day, I called for Lisa-Lotte and we walked together to Clare's. Lisa-Lotte had the yellow bathing suit and her bathing cap and the little rubber bathing shoes her mother made her wear in the water all neatly rolled up in a towel. I was wearing my bath-

ing suit, my old gray one with the stretched-out seat,
under my shorts, and I had the raggedy pink bath
towel I always took to the pool slung over my shoulder. I purposely forgot my bathing cap so I could
break the rules and swim without one. I hated the
way it felt to have anything tight like that on my
head. Clare was waiting outside for us. "Darlene can't
go," she said. "She's got a headache."

"This is Lisa-Lotte," I said to Clare. Lisa-Lotte
held out her hand, in that way she had of being man-
nerly without showing off. Clare looked surprised,
then interested, and shook hands.

"Lisa-Lotte," Clare said. "That's a pretty name."

"It's German," I explained. "Lisa-Lotte and her
parents had to run away from Hitler." Clare nodded.
"They're lucky they weren't killed," I went on. "It
was really close."

Clare looked at Lisa-Lotte, who was walking with
her shoulders hunched. "If I was smart enough to get
away from Hitler," Clare said cheerfully, "I'd stand
up straight, no matter what." She stood up straight
and stuck out her chest. "Ahem!" she said loudly, to
make sure Lisa-Lotte looked at her.

Lisa-Lotte giggled and straightened up. So did I.

Clare was wearing a white shirt and a powder blue
skirt. She was carrying a canvas swimming bag with
bright stripes running all around it. Inside, it turned
out, she had a black two-piece swimsuit, a brand-
new-looking white towel, a bathing cap, soap and
shampoo, a hairbrush and a comb, a pale pink lipstick, and some baby oil mixed with iodine, for getting

a suntan. She had as much stuff with her as my mother did, the once a year my father and I talked her into going with us to the pool.

Just about all the way to the park, I had trouble staying on the sidewalk. There didn't seem to be room enough for three kids to walk together anymore. The first thing I thought was, we must really be getting bigger. And then I thought it was Clare's jam-packed swimming bag taking up what should have been my space. And then I thought it was the way she walked, swinging her hips sideways instead of just going forward.

But then I got the feeling that Clare was doing it on purpose. So I crowded up as close as I could to Lisa-Lotte, who was in the middle, and I just didn't let myself get pushed off onto the grass. And Clare crowded up close to Lisa-Lotte on the other side, and just didn't let herself be pushed off, either. Of course, Lisa-Lotte got squished in between us, and every time my sweaty arm touched her sweaty arm, our arms stuck together.

When I got tired of shoving, I walked on the grass. "That sidewalk is burning hot," I said. "It's burning my feet right through my shoes. The grass is a lot cooler. You guys should walk on the grass."

Lisa-Lotte and Clare spread out on the sidewalk, so there was space between them. Neither one of them joined me on the grass.

I tried walking ahead. "Come on," I called impatiently. "We're never going to get there if you don't walk up."

Finally, when we were close enough to the pool to smell chlorine and hear kids screaming, I skipped down to the end of the street and waited for them at the corner.

In the ladies' dressing room, Lisa-Lotte and Clare each stepped into a private stall and closed the doors behind them. I dumped my towel on the bench in the open, public part of the room, just like always. Then I tore off my shorts and my T-shirt, threw them and my shoes into one of the wire baskets, grabbed the pin with my basket number on it and stuck it onto my bathing suit. I waited impatiently at the counter outside the dressing room until Lisa-Lotte and Clare came out, together. Then I slid the basket with my clothes and shoes in it across the counter to the boys working there, called, "Last one in is a rotten egg," and ran for the pool, splashing as hard as I could through the warm footbath full of smelly disinfectant. I cannonballed into the deep end, creating a big enough splash to make one of the lifeguards blow a warning whistle at me.

When I surfaced and looked around, I saw that neither Lisa-Lotte nor Clare had followed me. So I paddled to the side, hauled myself up out of the water, and went to find them. They were still inside, just leaning against the counter and talking to the high-school boys who checked the baskets in and out. "This is my friend," I heard Clare say. "Her name's Lisa."

Lisa-Lotte and Clare rubbed the oil mixed with iodine on each other's backs and lay down in the sun. I didn't want any of that stuff on me. I spread my towel next to theirs and tried sunbathing for a few minutes. But the hot sun made me itch, and lying there made me nervous.

"Let's play water tag," I proposed.

Clare didn't answer. "Later I will," said Lisa-Lotte, tilting her chin up and not opening her eyes.

"I'm going in," I said.

"Have fun," Clare answered, turning from her stomach to her back and reaching for the oil.

"You guys'll get burned," I warned. Neither one of them moved. "Okay," I said, "I'm going in."

I got on line for the high dive. Most of the kids waiting there were smaller than I, bony and restless. As usual, there was a lot of pushing going on. But it was worth putting up with, for the fun of jumping off the high dive.

When I was halfway up the ladder, someone shoved me, and without looking, I kicked back at them, the whole time keeping my eye on the person ahead of me, to make sure I wouldn't get kicked. When it was finally my turn, I walked out to the end of the rough, springy board and bounced up and down a couple of times. Then I walked back and took the regulation three steps to the end of the board, as if I intended to spring-dive. I knew how. I did it off the low boards all the time.

Then I walked back again and started over. The kids waiting behind me began to yell. They wanted me to hurry up and take my turn so they could have theirs. I wanted to take my time. In the end, I just ran as fast as I could and jumped, holding my nose with one hand and reaching for the sky with the other.

Then I was under the water. My feet touched the pale blue bottom of the pool. I pushed up off it and kicked, holding my breath and heading for the light.

After you jumped off the high board, you had to get out of the way in a hurry so the next kid didn't jump in on top of you and break your neck. That had happened one summer. It was a long time ago, but my father warned me about it. You never know what kind of fool is coming behind you, he said.

I swam over to the side and hung on. Clare was up on one elbow. "I thought you were going to dive," she said.

"I dive off the low board," I told her.

"Why not the high one?" she asked.

"It's more fun to jump," I lied.

Clare shrugged. "I can swan-dive off the high board," she said.

"Really?" Lisa-Lotte asked, sitting up and tugging at her swimsuit to make sure it covered her.

Clare nodded. "Want to see?"

I climbed out and stood over the two of them, shaking my wet hair and splattering water on them. "Stop it!" "Quit!" they both squealed, but they were laughing.

"What's a swan dive?" Lisa-Lotte wanted to know.

"Like this," I said, standing on one foot and mimicking one, with my eyes closed and my neck stretched out, making the graceful dive seem like something clownish.

1944

"I'll show you," Clare said. She stood and slowly pulled on her white bathing cap. She pushed every last hair up under it. Stalling, I thought. Then she strolled over to the high dive, where she had to wait her turn. Little kids jostled all around her, but Clare didn't seem to notice them, and she climbed step by step to the diving board without getting kicked or kicking anyone. Lisa-Lotte and I watched.

Some boys ahead of her got into a fight, and the lifeguard blew his whistle and motioned for them to get down. "Off the steps," he called. The rest of the kids in line swung over to the sides of the ladder to let the wild little boys scramble down.

Now the lifeguard and nearly everybody else was looking at the high dive, and it was Clare's turn.

She gracefully took three steps and pushed off the end of the board, getting just enough spring to do a quick swan and plunge into the water at an angle.

Then she sidestroked over to the stairs at the deep end, climbed out, and strolled back to where Lisa-Lotte and I were sitting. She took off her bathing cap, fluffed her hair out with her fingers, and sat back down on her towel.

"That's a swan dive," she told Lisa-Lotte.

I knew if I tried a swan dive with all those people watching and hit the water at an angle like that—in danger of doing a belly flop—I'd be so embarrassed I'd stay in the pool until everyone went back to what they were supposed to be doing and forgot all about me. But Clare didn't seem to understand that her dive hadn't been very good.

I watched Clare and Lisa-Lotte roast for a few minutes, and then I went back into the water. I played tag for a while with some kids I knew from school. And after they left, I practiced swimming underwater until I made it all the way from one side to the other.

On the way back, the sidewalk was so hot you could have fried an egg on it, so I walked on the grass, and they did, too.

On Saturday, we got the letter I'd been waiting for, the letter from Uncle Bob, from France.

"I'm here at last." he wrote. "The weather is awful. Even if the days are nice, which most of them aren't, the nights are freezing cold. I'm wearing long underwear and three sweaters and I'm still cold. In summer!

"This countryside is divided into little square fields separated by hedgerows," he wrote. "The hedgerows have been here forever and are about ten feet thick and four feet high, with trees and bushes growing right out of the top of them. In every one of them, German soldiers might be hiding.

"For a couple of days some of my buddies and I got to stay in a deserted farmhouse, which we made into a communications center. The house had holes in it from bullets and shrapnel and a caved-in roof. But it was swell to have shelter.

"It's funny," he wrote, "when you're moving out into enemy territory and you don't know when they are going to start shooting at you, you keep wanting to pull up close to the guy ahead. The lieutenant keeps yelling to spread out. So we spread out. But the next thing you know, there you are up close again.

"You'd think we'd have learned not to do it after Anderson stepped on that mine and Frank Bartlett, who was too close, got hurt pretty bad by flying body parts, but you just bunch up when you're scared," he wrote. "It's the natural thing to do, I guess."

"Body parts," my mother said in a confused way.

"War, Rosemary," my dad said gently.

Usually Dad would leave Uncle Bob's letters on the table in the kitchen, underneath the salt shaker, so we could read them again when we felt like it. This one he folded up and tucked into the pocket of his shirt.

I thought about running over to tell Dan that Uncle Bob was finally there, in France, at the party. But I decided to wait. There didn't seem to be any particular reason to hurry.

THIRTEEN

*N*ow, after supper, boys came and stood around in front of Clare's. The slow-falling August nights were close and still and nearly as hot as the days. As it got dark, the tops of the trees seemed to melt together, to make a black canopy between the earth and the sky.

Little kids played kick the can or hide-and-seek. Inside their houses, people turned on lamps and radios. Screen doors slammed sharply, dishes clattered, water ran. The noisy cicadas crowded in.

Usually, after dinner, Dan went off on his bike, alone, and Eddie and Marvin had a lazy catch in Marvin's driveway, throwing just hard enough so the ball would make that satisfying *thwock* as it hit the pockets of their gloves, but not so hard that either of them would miss.

And goofy-looking boys came to stand around at Clare's.

Sometimes it was the two sunburned boys who worked at the pool, tall boys, their noses peeling, their voices darker than smaller boys' voices, rougher than men's.

They hung around on the steps in front of Clare's apartment building. But they didn't go inside. Clare invited them. "Come on inside," she said to the boys and to Lisa-Lotte and to me. "Okay," the boys said. But no one went in. Instead, we sat down on the steps.

"I thought we were going inside," I complained, swatting at the first squadron of mosquitoes.

Nobody answered me.

When boys were there, Clare smiled a lot. Lisa-Lotte blushed. The two of them and the boys talked, but I was never quite sure what anyone was saying. It was hard for me to concentrate on the odd talk that stopped and started and interrupted itself with laughter and with giggling and with throat-clearing.

I tried to listen, but it wasn't interesting, and I found myself thinking about going home. I wanted to leave but didn't know how to do it. So I just sat there, thinking about leaving, thinking about the heat.

"Hot," one of the boys said.

"Damn hot," agreed the other, boldly.

"Oooh," Clare warned.

"Sorry." He thought Clare was shocked by swearing. But when there weren't any boys around, Clare swore.

"It's too hot to sit here another minute," Clare

said, pushing the damp hair up off the back of her neck and letting it fall.

"Do that again," one boy said.

Clare lifted her hair. The boy leaned over and blew on the back of Clare's neck.

"Oh!" she cried, jumping up to hit him. He antici- pated her and dodged down off the steps and onto the sidewalk. She chased him. He ducked away and cir- cled back.

Clare could have caught him easily. But she didn't do it. She just made those silly passes, grabbing at his shirt, which was white and smelled like clean laundry right off the line.

"It's too hot," Clare said, standing on the sidewalk now. "Too hot, just to be sitting."

"Let's walk, then," one boy suggested.

"Okay," Clare agreed. Lisa-Lotte and I got up. I pulled at the back of my shorts, which were sticking to my legs because of the heat, and because of the hu- midity. That's one of the sayings people around here trade back and forth all summer, every summer. "It's not the heat," they say, "it's the humidity."

"Hot," they say. "It's hot."

"Hot enough for you?" they ask.

"Boy, it's hot."

"I bet I could cook an egg right here on the side- walk."

"It sure is hot."

"Come on," the boy said.

We started out as slowly as people moving under- water.

1944

Soon we were a group, walking together. The boys walked next to each other. Lisa-Lotte and Clare were behind. It was like the day we walked to the pool. There was only enough room on the sidewalk for people to walk in twos. The third person had to walk on the curb or on the grass, or hang back. I walked on the grass, next to Clare, who smelled of White Shoulders toilet water. Her mother's.

The boys jostled each other and laughed their cracked laughs. The next thing I knew, five of us were trying to walk together. Then we were back to twos, but switched around, with one of the croaky boys walking next to Lisa-Lotte and the other one walking next to Clare. I tried again to listen to the conversation, but there were two conversations now. And I couldn't quite hear either one of them.

And then I saw that Lisa-Lotte was holding hands with the one boy and Clare was holding hands with the other. And there were no conversations.

"Watch this!" I said, cartwheeling down the sidewalk ahead of them and waiting at the end of the block with my hands on my hips.

They drifted toward me, through the hot night, the one white shirt glowing in the almost-dark. They were holding hands and walking. I was standing alone at the end of the block, watching them come. I wanted to die.

"I'm going home!" I called.

As I took off, Dan appeared on his bike. He rode in the street next to them, wobbling in order to go as slowly on the bike as they were walking. They all talked together, but I was too far away by then to hear a thing they said. I could only hear my own breathing as I ran, and my own crying.

When I got home, I went around back. I didn't want my parents to know I was upset. But my father was there, standing on the porch in the dark with his foot up on the rail, smoking a cigarette and staring into space.

I sat down on the stairs and wiped the tears and sweat off my face with my hands. My father and I both stared out into the darkness.

"What's the matter, El?" he asked.

"Nothing."

"Mmm."

"It's those kids."

"Those kids don't mean a thing," my father said. "They won't mean a thing to you one day.

"You've got your whole life ahead of you," he said. "You're going to go way beyond them. They won't mean anything to you, later. Things change, you know."

I didn't feel like arguing with my father, but I knew he was wrong. They would always mean something.

Lisa-Lotte called me up when she got home. "Where did you go?" she asked. "Why did you leave? We just walked around the block," she told me. "And then we all went to Clare's and played records. Dan came, too. We tried to teach the boys how to jitterbug." She giggled. "Impossible!" she said. "Why did you leave, Ellen?"

"You were holding hands," I accused.

1944

"Oh, not so much," she said. "Come over to Clare's tomorrow," she said. "We're going to try a new way to curl hair. With rags." Lisa-Lotte was feeling bad. "You will come?"

"I'll see," I told her. "Maybe."

I didn't want to curl my hair with rags. I would go crazy, sleeping on rags.

"Please?" Lisa-Lotte was determined. "Clare told me to ask you, for sure to invite you."

"Okay." I relented halfheartedly.

I could hear Lisa-Lotte smiling as she said, "Good." She seemed relieved, and I wondered if Mrs. Siegel had said she couldn't go to Clare's if I didn't.

Lisa-Lotte was never by herself anymore. Clare gave her a peach-colored silk scarf (Clare had a blue one), and the two of them walked around the neighborhood, wearing scarves. Scarves, on the dog-hot August afternoons, when the the stiff weeds had pushed right up through the sidewalks and the white dust had coated every leaf on every tree and nobody else went out if they could help it, and nothing stirred.

My mother laughed. "Must be awful hot with a silk scarf around your head on a day like this," she said.

I didn't answer.

"That's the way it is," she went on. "Girls'll do anything to look pretty."

"They look stupid," I said.

My mother pretended to be surprised. "Who's jealous?" she said.

"I am not jealous," I told her. "I would not go

around in the heat wearing a damn silk scarf if I had one."

"Mind your tongue," she said mildly.

"Well, I wouldn't."

She sighed. "Maybe not. But there isn't anything wrong with them doing it. They're not hurting anyone."

"They're hurting me!" I shouted, surprising both of us.

"They are not. If anybody's hurting you, it's you."

"*They* are hurting me," I insisted.

"Just how?" she wanted to know.

"By being mean and stuck-up."

"Fiddle," Mom said. "Ellen, you are just too used to having Lisa—"

"Lisa-Lotte," I interrupted.

"Lisa, she wants it to be Lisa now," Mom went on. "You're just accustomed to having Lisa at your beck and call, and you don't anymore. A girl needs to have more than one friend, anyway. There's no reason in the world the three of you can't be friends, except that you're so stubborn. Come on, now." She gave me a little hug. "Why don't you walk on over to Clare's and see what they're doing? Just go over and be friendly, and don't complain about everything. Go on."

She gently shoved me out the door, into the blazing afternoon. "The three of you can come back here later," she said. "I'll make us a pitcher of sun tea."

Sun tea was tea that you made by leaving a pitcher of water with tea bags in it out in the sun. And then you poured it over ice cubes and put a fresh mint leaf on top. My mother thought sun tea was a treat. It tasted just like any other kind of tea to me, but I never told her so.

I shuffled down the street, with my toes inside my shoes and my heels breaking down the backs. Boy, it was hot. Dog days. Days no better than dogs. Some of the boys Clare and Lisa-Lotte knew thought I was a dog. What would my mother say if I told her that? "Just be sweet," she'd probably say. "You be sweet, now, Ellen."

I wondered what Uncle Bob would say.

I wrote to him in my head as I shuffled along the blistering sidewalk. "Dear Uncle Bob, A new girl named Clare is Lisa-Lotte's best friend now. They walk around with silk scarves on, looking for boys."

What kind of a letter would that be to write to a soldier far away from home? No kind. I knew better. I knew that you never wrote to a serviceman telling him anything that wasn't cheerful or anything that would make him worry. You didn't want him worrying when he needed to concentrate on winning the war and not getting himself killed while he was at it.

It wasn't right to complain about anything anyway, when there was a war, while people who weren't even soldiers were being shot and starved and bombed and murdered. That's what my dad said. "Murdered, for no reason."

"Quit complaining about every little thing, Ellen," my mother said. "When you feel like complaining, just stop for a minute and think about the war. Think about all those people who are just like us getting driven out of their homes and shot dead if they complain about it. Think about that when you feel like complaining. That's what I do.

"Think about the war and you'll see you don't have one thing to complain about," she added.

I had plenty to complain about. Sometimes I couldn't wait until the damn war was over, so I could complain about all the things that made me mad and hurt my feelings. I was tired of being a saint.

Clare and Lisa-Lotte were wearing men's long white shirts over just their underwear. They were barefoot. They were gliding back and forth in Clare's living room, carrying books on their heads. I plopped down on the couch and watched them. When the book slid off, they would catch it and go back to the beginning, which was one end of the living-room rug, and start over. The idea was to go from one end of the room to the other and then back again without the book falling off.

"What're you doing that for?" I asked.

When they talked with the books on their heads, they barely moved their mouths, so it was hard to understand what they were saying. I waited until Clare's book fell off and asked again.

"We're improving our posture," Clare said.

Lisa-Lotte lost her book and didn't catch it. It landed right next to her bare toes. I wished it had cracked them.

"Try it," Clare said. She handed me a book. "Start over there," she said.

1944

I kicked off my shoes and went to the other side of the room. Then I put the book on my head and walked quickly to the end of the rug and back again. Lisa-Lotte and Clare watched. I took the book off my head. "Now what should we do?" I asked sarcastically.

"You didn't do it right," Clare said. "Watch me." She set her book back on her head and started out, taking long, gliding steps, like an ice skater. The book slipped off and she caught it. "You took itty baby steps," she said. "Anyone can do that."

"I took regular steps," I argued.

"Try again, Ellen," Lisa-Lotte said.

"No thanks."

After they practiced gliding with books on their heads for a while longer, we went into Clare's room, where they lay with their heads hanging over the side of the bed and brushed their hair, a hundred strokes. They counted and brushed together. I watched. When they sat up, their hair was full of electricity and sticking out around their heads, and their faces were red. Lisa-Lotte offered me her hairbrush when she was finished. "No thanks," I told her.

"When you get home," she advised, "a hundred strokes, two times each day. For healthy hairs."

"Hair," Clare corrected.

"Hair," said Lisa-Lotte.

"My hair is plenty healthy," I told her, tossing it out of my eyes and replacing the old barrette I kept it back with.

"It doesn't look all that healthy to me," Clare said. "It's kind of limp."

"It's healthy," I told her, glaring into her turquoise eyes. She shrugged.

After they rolled up each other's hair in rags, they started getting out the manicure stuff.

I sat on the end of my spine on the bedroom chair pretending to read *Tom Sawyer*. I'd read it before. And I didn't like it the first time.

"My mom is making sun tea," I said finally, getting up. "Come over later if you want some. I'm going to Dan's to check on the war."

"The war is going to be over in about five minutes," Clare called after me. "What are you going to think about then?"

FOURTEEN

*D*an was in the map room. I'd convinced him we would never be able to follow Uncle Bob through Europe. "We won't know *exactly* where he's been until he's moved on," I'd pointed out. "Let's just follow some of the Americans and pretend we know it's Uncle Bob. It'll be more interesting."

Dan actually agreed. I brought over letters we'd received from Uncle Bob after he got to France, so Dan could get him started and go on from there.

In an early letter, Uncle Bob wrote: "We are fighting field by field, and every single field is surrounded by hedgerows, which I think I told you about. We dig in and lie down all day and fight in the dark. The Germans are done for, but they keep on fighting. It's too close for artillery or tanks. It's all up to the dough in a situation like this."

"The dough?" I'd asked.

"Foot soldiers," my father had told me. "Dough-boys."

The next letter said: "The krauts are dug in behind hedges and hiding in ditches. If we used planes or heavy guns, we would kill ourselves. Every once in a while we come to a little town. Then we have to watch out for snipers. There are fewer cows to begin with in this part of the country, so there are not so many dead ones lying around."

The next letter was shorter. "We are moving so fast now, we get ahead of our supplies. Then we have to wait. But I bet I will be home by Christmas anyway."

Uncle Bob sent some pictures of himself. In one of them, he stood in front of a broken stone wall. The sun was in his eyes, so the way he bent his head toward the camera and half smiled made him look very bashful. He had his jacket open and his hands stuck in his pants pockets. Right behind him, you could see a pile of wires and some broken two-by-fours and what looked like the inside of a house. You could see the top of the walls, but no ceilings, and you could see the torn-up flowered wallpaper.

Dan and I felt giddy as we pretended to track Uncle Bob. After years of treating the maps as if they were pages right out of the Bible, Dan began to be silly. He drew pencil pictures of dead cows with their four legs up in the air all over France. And we tried to make a money bet with Eddie that Uncle Bob's unit would be the first to get to Paris, but Eddie had found out that we weren't sure which unit Uncle Bob really was with, and wanted to know what kind of fool did we take him for?

We tried it on Marvin, but Eddie had warned him.

I bragged about the war to my father. But he wouldn't get excited yet. "We'll see," he said.

"You know the Germans are beaten," I argued. "They just won't admit it yet. Listen to the news," I advised him. "It will all be over any minute."

"We'll see" was all he'd say.

"Your father doesn't want to get his hopes up," Mom told me.

"But, Mom, Uncle Bob is probably going to be home for Christmas!"

She put her arms around me and squeezed. "I know," she whispered. "Isn't it wonderful?"

Summer ended, and we eighth-graders all went back to school in high spirits. We were the oldest kids in the school at last. We were publishing the school newspaper and standing guard at the crosswalks. We were monitoring the hallways and working in the school cafeteria. We were running the talent show. We were first string on all the intramural teams. At Christmas, we would have all the biggest parts and all the solos in the Christmas pageant. And this year, our fathers and brothers and uncles and cousins and family friends who had been fighting in Europe would be there to see us. We were sure they would all be home for Christmas.

But it turned out we were wrong and my father was right. On December 16, 1944, Uncle Bob and thousands of other Allied soldiers were surprised by a German counterattack in Belgium, where the Germans broke right through the American lines. It was called the Battle of the Bulge.

My father swore under his breath. "Here we go again," he said out loud.

After that, we got only short letters from Uncle Bob, and they didn't come very often.

"Before the Bulge," he wrote, "we chopped down a fir tree for Christmas and decorated it with hand grenades. We didn't know we would need them like we do."

"Weather's bitter. All ice and snow and fog. Germans do not give up. You think you can't take another step. But you don't want to let your buddies down."

"Sometimes you don't know where the Germans are," he wrote. "You can't see anything. And you can't tell from the sounds of the guns, because both sides use each other's captured weapons. Sometimes we fire on our own troops or they fire on us. Yesterday we dodged American bullets all day. Mostly the radio was dead, so we couldn't tell anyone."

"How did that get by the censor?" my father wondered.

"It seems like stuff gets by," I observed, "as long as he doesn't say exactly where it happened."

"We haven't changed clothes for weeks," Bob wrote, "or had a bath or a hot meal. When you go into a house the Germans just left, you don't touch the picture of Hitler hanging on the wall or a booby trap will go off and kill a couple of guys. That happened to us."

"The Germans fight until they see there's no hope," he wrote, "and then they pull and run and we go after them. We leave nothing but rubble behind us. Stone houses completely destroyed. And burned-out tanks in the middle of the road. And men all over the place who died such a short time ago they still look like they're just sleeping.

"The nights are cold," he wrote. "And we are tired."

1945

FIFTEEN

*M*y eighth-grade year and the war in Europe were both almost over. Time, which had passed so slowly for so long—for my whole life—had speeded up. Suddenly I was having a wild ride.

"My life is like a runaway horse," I announced dramatically at the beginning of a letter to Uncle Bob that I imagined but never got around to writing, "and I don't take after Mom's cousin Vicky, after all."

Flat-as-a-board Vicky and I had nothing in common, it turned out. But I wasn't encumbered the way Lisa was, either. "Encumber." That was one of the words I had to spell and define in the county-wide spelling bee, in front of eighth-graders from five different schools, and parents, and teachers. Richard Heller and I represented our class. Richard was knocked out early, by the word "indict." I got all the way through "encumber." The word I missed was "exhilarate." Because of "exhilarate," I came in third.

Anyway, by the time I was getting to the end of the eighth grade and the U.S.A. was getting to the end of the war in Europe, I had breasts that fit and weren't any trouble. My only worry in that department was that mine might not be finished yet, since the rest of me wasn't. I was almost five foot six, and my dad was sure I'd grow at least another inch, because my feet were so big.

"Where in the world did she get all that height from?" my mother asked, looking at me as if I were getting too big on purpose.

"She gets it from my side," Dad answered proudly. "Same as Bobby. Nothing wrong with height," he added. "Gives you a leg-up in the world."

"Nothing wrong with height," Mom said, "for a man."

"I don't know why you say things like that," my father scolded. "She's healthy and straight and strong. And tall. She's fine."

Easy for him to say, but I didn't always think being tall was fine. I was taller than everyone's mother and even taller than my eighth-grade teacher, the horrible Miss Henderson. What's more, most of the cute boys in the world came up to about my waist. Richard Heller was an exception. He had a growth spurt after Christmas and now, if I stood with my knees bent just a little, we were eye to eye.

Lisa complained that walking with me made her

feel like a midget. "Well, walking next to you makes me feel like a giant," I told her.

"Feeling like a midget is worse," she said.

"Wrong!" I argued. "How would you like to be as tall as I am and still growing?"

"Well . . ." She backed off as politely as she could. "Maybe not that tall. But somewhere in between would be nice. Like Clare."

I agreed with Lisa. I thought Clare was perfect. But in the middle of an argument, I wasn't going to admit it.

"I don't know," I said. "It would probably be worse to be Miss Average. Nobody wants to be just average."

"I do," Lisa said frankly. "I would be much happier being average."

"Well, you're not," I said, "so you might as well forget it. You're not average in any way. You're above-average smart and below-average tall, and you've got enormous boobs, which are anything but average—"

Lisa shoved me hard. "Shut up for once, Ellen," she said.

Uncle Bob didn't make it home for Christmas, or for Easter, either. The letters we got from him came from "somewhere in Germany" now. They were short, as if he'd written them in a hurry or as if he just didn't have much to say to us.

He wrote: "The Germans destroy the church steeples so we can't use them for observation posts."

That reminded me of a finger game we played when

I was little: "This is the church, this is the steeple, open the doors and see all the people." Now the churches had no steeples, and probably no doors, either. And what had happened to the people?

He wrote: "We are picking up German propaganda broadcasts on the radio. Someone named Anna, a Nazi who speaks English like an American. She makes fun of us and threatens us. She gives false news reports that are hard not to believe. Right at sundown, she tells us our own new secret password, even though it is changed every night."

"German soldiers are surrendering now," Uncle Bob wrote. "Most of them are young, some only fifteen or sixteen years old. They are hungry and scared."

Then we got the photograph. The note that came with it just said: "Me and my buddies." The picture showed two new graves marked by crosses made out of broken boards. The photographer was standing with the sun behind him and his long shadow spread across the graves. The shadow was Uncle Bob's.

Mom gasped when she saw the picture and then glanced at me, to see if I had looked already or not. Dad studied it and reread the note. "Pray Bobby gets wounded soon," he finally said. "Or else he's going to get killed."

Pray for Uncle Bob to be wounded! Right at the very end of the war? I could not believe my father had even thought such a thing, let alone said it out loud. All these years, wishing for Uncle Bob to be safe, and now his own brother could say a thing like that.

"Frank!" Mom exclaimed.

Dad crumpled up the note in his fist and held it toward her. "I'm telling you," he said fiercely, "it's as clear as day, if he doesn't get wounded and sent to the rear, he's not going to make it."

He threw the note onto the kitchen table and slammed out of the house. My mother nervously smoothed the crumpled page. I stared at the photograph. At the graves. At the tall shadow that was all I could see of Uncle Bob.

"Your father's upset," Mom said. "He didn't mean it. It's the war. Going on and on and on. Don't pay any attention. Your father doesn't want Bob hurt, you know that."

I didn't see any point in arguing with her. But I knew my father had meant what he said.

Uncle Bob wrote: "We are very, very careful now. Nobody wants to be the last one killed."

Clare and Darlene had started getting regular letters, too. Theirs were from Clare's father in California. "The air here in Los Angeles is full of the smell of orange blossoms," he wrote them. "Everything in California is fresh and beautiful, just like the two of you."

Clare was happy. I never guessed how much she'd missed her father. Now she talked about him all the time. He knew a million card tricks and two million jokes. He knew the tunes and the words to every popular song that had ever been written. He'd been a singer and a comedian in vaudeville when he was young. His name was Harry. Harry Darling. We made it into a joke. Darlene and Clare and Lisa and I called him Harry-darling, never just Harry, when we talked about him.

Harry-darling's letters and long-distance telephone calls worked like magic, and he and Darlene were reconciled. That's the way Clare put it. "They're reconciled," she said. "They're getting back together. As soon as school is out, Darlene and I are moving to California!"

I hated to lose Clare just when she and I had gotten to be real friends. But she and Darlene were so happy it was catching, and I ended up feeling happy, too.

"We want you guys to come visit," Clare told Lisa and me, "as soon as we get settled. Well, as soon as the war is over.

"We'll go to the corner of Hollywood and Vine, and watch the stars come out." Clare giggled. She was quoting Harry-darling. "We'll go to Grauman's Chinese Theatre and see the famous footprints," she said, "and swim in the Pacific Ocean. And then we'll stroll around until we're spotted by talent scouts and we'll all end up in the movies!"

Nothing would be able to keep me from visiting Clare and Darlene and Harry-darling in Los Angeles, "the City of Angels," Darlene translated.

"And of movie stars," Clare added, batting her eyelids.

But Lisa probably wouldn't come to Los Angeles to visit, she told Clare. "My parents would worry too much."

1945

"You're going to have to go someplace without them someday," Clare said.

Lisa didn't answer, and I got the feeling she might not be able to go where she wanted to, even someday, that she might not think she should, if it meant she had to leave her parents and worry them.

A few nights after that picture came from Uncle Bob, I slept over at Clare's, and Darlene was home. We ate hot dogs and baked beans cold out of a can, and carrot sticks. Clare and I had Cokes and Darlene drank a beer. I didn't know any other woman who drank beer. I'd seen one once, while I was looking out the window of a bus. She was a tired-seeming woman sitting on the stoop of a sagging house with her feet, in shapeless old men's shoes, set wide apart on the stair. She was drinking beer right out of the bottle.

Darlene let me have a sip of hers, which she'd poured into a glass. I liked the foam, but not the taste.

After dinner, I told Clare and Darlene about the picture we got from Uncle Bob. And the note. And what my father thought. "I sure wish I could see your uncle's hand," Darlene said. She had a beer-foam mustache that she licked at and then wiped on her wrist. "If I could see his hand, I could tell you if his Lifeline is long or short."

"Which one is the Lifeline?" I asked.

"Let me look at your hand," she said.

I gave it to her, and she held it up close to her face and peered at my palm.

"Jesus, Mary, and Joseph!" she swore.

"What, Darlene?" Clare leaned over us so she could see.

"What?" I begged.

"Well, I mean . . ." Darlene hesitated. "I just have never seen such a—short—Lifeline," she said. "It just took me by surprise."

"Short?" I echoed. "Short? Are you sure?"

Darlene took a swallow of her beer and looked again. "Well, honey, I hate to tell you, but there it is. See, it starts down here . . ." She traced a line on the palm of my hand with the tip of one of her polished nails. "And it ends—right—here."

Darlene squeezed my hand and gave it back to me. "Better live hard, honey," she advised.

I felt stunned. It wasn't Uncle Bob who was going to be unlucky and die young. It was me!

"Which hand did you give her, El?" Clare asked.

"This one." I held it up.

"I thought you were right-handed."

"I am."

"That's your left hand, dodo."

"So?"

"So it doesn't count. Show Darlene your right one."

I looked at Darlene, who nodded and reached for my other hand. It was hard for me to let her see it and maybe find out I was going to die next week, but I did.

"Well, that's more like it!" Darlene said.

"It is?" I asked.

"You bet it is," she said. "Look here, this one starts way down here, practically on your wrist, and then it

curves around all the way up to under your index finger. Girl, you are probably going to live to be a hundred!" I realized I'd been holding my breath, and I let
it out.

"Live hard anyway," Clare said, laughing. "This
isn't foolproof."

"Oh, you," said Darlene. "Don't listen to her,
Ellen. She's just teasing. Why, now we've seen the
right hand, you can live as slow as molasses. You'll
have time for everything."

V-E Day came on May 8, 1945. The war in Europe
was over at last. A bunch of little kids in our neighborhood paraded around after school, banging pot lids
together and beating on pans with spoons, singing
and hollering. They sang that silly song kids had been
singing since the war began about spitting in the
Führer's face. They sang "The Star-Spangled Ban-
ner." And they stood by the side of the road screaming, "God bless America!" at the passing cars.

At the meeting that night of the eighth-grade
Graduation Party Committee, everyone was in high
spirits. Richard Heller walked all the way home
with Clare and Lisa and me, and after we dropped
them off, he tried to kiss me, twice. Of course, I
didn't let him, but I was glad he tried. I thought
maybe I would let him, after the graduation party.
But I wasn't sure. It might be more fun to almost let
him, the way I had been, than it would be to actually go through with it.

We got a letter from Uncle Bob a couple of weeks

later, about V-E Day. "I sat right by the radio while Churchill talked," he wrote. "I didn't want to miss a word. I was thinking, 'The war is over, and I am still alive.' Guys all around me were cheering, and some of them were crying. And I was thinking, 'The war is over,' and not feeling much of anything."

"Bobby's hurt," my father said. He had tears in his eyes.

Mom grabbed his hand and looked up into his face. "Bob's alive!" she cried. "He's alive and he's in one piece and he's coming home!" It was as if she was begging my father for something. "Listen to me," she said. "He's coming home. It's all that matters."

I read the letter again. "The war is over, and I am still alive."

But the war wasn't over. The other war, the war in the Pacific, raged on. Dan told me once that after the war in Europe was through, everyone there wouldn't just get to come home and be done with it. A lot of the soldiers in Europe would be retrained and sent to fight in the Pacific. Knowing about this kept me from feeling completely happy. What if Uncle Bob was one of the ones who had to go on fighting?

"You're just like your father," my mother said, "always looking on the dark side. You're a pessimist. Shame on you!"

"I am not a pessimist," I retorted. "I am just not stupid!"

"Apologize to your mother!" my father ordered.

I apologized, but she cried anyway.

This wasn't the way I thought my parents and I

would act when the war was over. We had to be careful or we would have been quarreling all the time until
we heard. But once we knew that Uncle Bob was not
going on to the Pacific, that he would be coming
home, mustered out of the Army and sent back to be a
civilian no matter how long the other part of the war
went on, we all felt better and calmed down.

It wasn't just luck that was getting Uncle Bob out.
It was because he'd been overseas for so long and had
seen so much active duty, he'd accumulated a whole
lot more points than you needed to get out instead of
being retrained.

He would be coming home, but not right away.
There was "mopping up" to take care of first. There
were snipers, there were nuts who wouldn't give up,
and there were even some German soldiers who
wouldn't believe their leaders had surrendered, and
they kept on fighting.

Uncle Bob wrote: "Sometimes I think if I hear one
more shot or see one more dead person, I will go
nuts."

Clare and Darlene moved to California the week
after graduation, in the middle of June. Richard
Heller moved away, too. I was sorry I hadn't let him
kiss me. We had come so close, I'd felt his minty
breath. But at the last second, I stood up straight, and
that threw him off his mark. If he'd kept leaning toward me, he would have kissed my chin.

Lisa spent the summer taking sewing classes at the
Singer sewing machine company. I worked as a junior

counselor at the new coed recreation program, which ran until August.

And then Uncle Bob came home.

Uncle Bob's train was late, of course. Trains were always late, crowded and dirty and late, ever since the beginning of the war. So by the time Dad and Uncle Bob got to the house and Mom and I watched them climb out of the Buick, I felt out of sorts, as if I'd been waiting for a week instead of just most of a hot August day.

Mom ran out to the car and hugged Uncle Bob. Dad got his gear out of the trunk. And I stood leaning in the doorway, with one bare foot on top of the other, and watched the three of them come up the front walk.

My mother had her arm around Uncle Bob's waist, and she was beaming up at him. His face was tilted down toward her. My father walked behind them, lugging the duffel bag. And I stood and watched, and waited for Uncle Bob to look up and see me.

But when he did lift his head, finally, his eyes looked like Lisa's do when she's reading and you interrupt her and she looks up from her book and doesn't know you. That's the way Uncle Bob's eyes were when he looked at me. He didn't really see me. He wasn't back yet. I could tell.

"Welcome home, Uncle Bob," I said. It sounded wrong. Small. It wasn't nearly enough to say. But it was all I could think of, and he didn't seem to notice.

"Hey, kiddo," he said, putting one arm around my shoulder in a clumsy hug as he went by.

1945

He looked around the dim front hallway (the whole house was dim, closed up tight against the sun) and tossed his cap onto the table. Then he took the duffel from my dad and went slowly up the stairs into his old room, and closed the door. He must have gone to sleep, because we didn't see him again until the next afternoon when he came out and just stood, in his undershirt and his khaki pants and his dog tags, and looked around him as if he had found himself dropped down on a strange planet and had no idea what he should do next.

Uncle Bob didn't want a welcome-home party, but my dad told him he didn't think there was much choice. "Rosemary has the bit between her teeth," Dad said.

Mom wanted to invite a lot of people who knew Bob and would be happy to see him again. But he said he couldn't deal with that. "Just the neighbors, then," she coaxed. "Otherwise, we'll have people lurking around the house trying to catch a glimpse of you, the way we did yesterday!" Mom laughed, but I could tell Uncle Bob felt upset.

"It was just some of the kids on the block," I explained. "Some boys. They're curious."

"Not curious, Ellen," Mom said. "Interested."

Anyway, even though Uncle Bob was reluctant, Mom went ahead with the party. She kept it small, just asked the neighbors over on Sunday afternoon. She didn't call any of Uncle Bob's old friends. She would leave that up to him to do when he felt like it, which she hoped, she told him, would be real soon.

I noticed Uncle Bob didn't answer Mom when she spoke to him like this, telling him how to behave. He didn't seem annoyed. He just ignored her. Or maybe he didn't even hear.

Mom got out the Christmas punch bowl with the matching ladle and the cups that hooked over the side. She put a block of orange sherbet in the bowl and poured ginger ale over it, to make punch. She baked oatmeal bars and brownies and made sandwiches with pink pimiento cheese spread, cut in triangles and arranged on top of paper doilies on cookie sheets.

That was it.

On our block, we weren't used to formal socializing, and most of the neighbors didn't stay long.

Things went pretty well, I guess.

Marvin and Eddie and Dan stood around Uncle Bob and peppered him with questions.

"How many of them did you get?" Eddie wanted to know.

"Get?" said Uncle Bob, frowning.

"Kill," Dan explained.

Uncle Bob kept on frowning. "Some," he said.

"Did you bring back a Luger," Marvin asked, "or anything?"

"No," Uncle Bob said.

"Nothing?" Eddie asked.

"Nothing," he answered.

Mrs. Siegel pushed her husband forward. He looked up at Uncle Bob. "My wife and I are wondering," he said carefully, "if you would not mind telling us. Did you see perhaps survivors of the concentration

camps? Did you meet someone from any of them?"
The Siegels had begun to search for missing relatives.

"No," Uncle Bob told Mr. Siegel quietly. "I heard
about it, but I didn't see anything."

"And nobody did you meet?" Mr. Siegel persisted.

Uncle Bob shook his head. "No," he said, "I'm
sorry."

Mrs. Anger waited, looking like a cat ready to
pounce on a mouse. She stood by herself, holding a
cup of frothy punch and a plate with a couple of sandwiches on it. "How in the world," she said finally,
"did you manage to get back in one piece, Bob
Parker, when there's so many didn't?"

Uncle Bob gave her a long, level look. "I can't ex-
plain it, Mrs. Anger," he said. Then he took himself
upstairs, just like that, and the party was over.

Lisa stayed to help clean up. "It's what's driving
my parents crazy, too," she confided. "Being survivors. 'Why are we alive when so many others like us
are dead?' They go around like that in circles, inside
their minds, all the time." Lisa shook her head and
sighed.

"You'd think they'd just be thankful," Mom said.

"Yes," Lisa agreed politely. "But it's not so simple,
for them."

"Of course it isn't," Mom apologized.

"Sounds like the same kind of thing that's eating
Bob," my father said.

I don't know what I expected it to be like when
Uncle Bob came home. I never bothered imagining

the details. I guess I just thought it would be the same as it was before. How dumb can a person be? I mean, how *could* it be the same? I was a little kid when Uncle Bob left. Now I was starting high school. And he had been to war.

Uncle Bob slept and slept. After dark, he went for long walks, by himself. One morning, I saw him standing in his room, holding a photograph in his hand, staring into space, with tears running down his cheeks and his neck and soaking the front of his undershirt. He wasn't making noise or breathing hard. He was just standing and staring. The tears were just rolling out.

I went into his room and stood next to him, but he didn't seem to notice me. So I took the picture out of his hand and looked at it. It was the graves, with Uncle Bob's shadow falling over them. I touched his arm. "You have to forget all that now," I said.

Then I tried to give the picture back, but he didn't take it. So I set it down on top of his bureau, next to his pocket change and his keys, and I left.

A little while later, I heard the shower running. It ran for a long time. Much longer than it would take for the hot water to give out.

Uncle Bob didn't know what he wanted to do. He didn't want his old job back, he told my dad, that was for sure. He might go to college, he said. Or move out to the West Coast. Or start up some kind of business of his own. Or get a car and just drive around.

Whatever Uncle Bob said, my parents agreed with

him. It made me angry, the way they tried to humor him. But he didn't seem to mind, or really even to notice what they thought. Anyone could see that. After a while my dad caught on. "It's a big world out there, Bobby," he said. "And you're a grown man. You'll figure things out."

But my mother couldn't stop thinking we ought to be able to do something to help. If Uncle Bob went to sit in the yard, she'd shoo me out after him. "Go on out and talk to him," she'd whisper.

I'd go and sit down next to him, out in the back yard, where it was ninety degrees in the shade, and we would have a stupid conversation, all starts and stops.

"My friend Clare moved to Los Angeles," I told him.

"Clare?" he said.

"I'll be starting high school in a couple of weeks."

"High school." He shook his head.

I reached down and picked the widest blade of grass I could find and split it down the middle, to make a grass whistle.

"You're all grown up," Uncle Bob said.

"Not all."

"You grew up while I was gone, kiddo," he said. "And I did, too." Then he laughed the saddest laugh I'd heard.

I squawked the grass whistle and threw it away. "I can do palm-reading," I told him. "Darlene taught me."

He didn't answer right away. "Darlene?" he finally said.

"Clare's mom." No answer. "The ones who moved to California."

"Oh, yeah."

Suddenly I felt inspired. "Let me look at your hand, Uncle Bob," I said. He didn't move. "Come on." I reached for the hand nearest to me.

He let me take it, and I turned it palm up. The lines ran every which way. I couldn't find any Lifeline at all, beginning, middle, or end. I should have practiced more on grownup hands, I guess. All I'd done were kids.

"Well!" I said.

"Well what?"

I stalled. "Well, this is pretty interesting."

"What is?"

I took a deep breath. "Well, see, here's your Lifeline, long and straight." I ran my finger quickly up and down his palm, hoping he wouldn't follow it. "But here's the interesting part," I improvised. "Here's your Journey line." I picked out a deep crease that cut across his palm. "You are about to take a journey that will change everything!"

Uncle Bob pulled his hand away. "I just did that, Ellen," he said.

I took it back. "That's not what I'm looking at," I said. "That one's down here, see?" I pointed to a crooked line, broken and crosshatched by others. "You can tell by all the stops and starts. That line is for the war. The one I mean is this one, see? This straight one up here. You can tell from where it is that it hasn't happened yet," I lied boldly. "That's because it's up here at the top of your hand. The war's down there at the bottom. It's over. You already did it. This is the one that counts now, this one up at the top."

Uncle Bob took back his hand. He didn't seem convinced.

"You *are* left-handed, aren't you?" I bluffed. I'd been looking at his left hand. If he was right-handed, I'd try again.

"Yes," he said.

"See?"

"A journey?" he asked.

"A meaningful journey," I told him.

"Not just a trip someplace?" he asked.

"A journey," I said firmly, by now almost believing it myself. "A journey. Much more important than a trip."

Finally Uncle Bob started doing things. He mowed in front and in back, and dug up every last bit of crabgrass out of the lawns. He propped up the fence. He washed all the windows, inside and out. He cleaned the basement and organized the garage. He didn't want help with any of it. He seemed angry every minute, and he worked like a demon.

Just about when he'd run out of work to do and I'd started to wonder what he'd do next, an Army buddy of his called him up. The buddy had an old car that he'd got running. The tires were still in good shape, and they'd be able to get gas along the way. "Nobody's going to tell a couple of vets like us they can't have gas for their car," he told Uncle Bob.

"It'll be our last mission," Uncle Bob told Mom and Dad and me.

He and his buddy were driving to South Dakota, to visit the wife of one of their friends who'd been killed. To tell her in person everything that had happened. They'd written to her and said they'd come if they could. She had a child her dead husband had never even had the chance to see. Uncle Bob and his buddy wanted to tell her everything, so she could tell the child, later on. So their friend wouldn't be forgotten.

Uncle Bob packed his things, and before we knew it, he was gone again.

"He was only here a month," Mom said.

Dad corrected her. "He was never here at all."

I knew that was right. When Uncle Bob left, his eyes were just as full of shadows as they were when he came.

"When he gets back, it'll be different," I told them.

My dad tried to rally. "Sure it will," he said.

"He didn't say when he was coming back," Mom reminded us. "Or if."

"He will come back," I assured her. "He just needs a little time, first."

For some reason, I was thinking of that photograph. Not the picture of the graves, but the snapshot Uncle Bob had sent from England a long time ago. The one of him and his buddy and the girl and the bike. I was remembering that Uncle Bob was the one with the girl.

1945

"He'll be back," I repeated, surprised at the confidence in my voice and the happiness I was feeling. I found myself wondering how old the child was, the one in South Dakota, whether it was a girl or a boy, and how long it would take Uncle Bob and the woman to figure out what I somehow already seemed to know.

"He'll be back," I repeated, "and everything will be all right."

My parents were impressed by my confidence. It seemed to make them feel better. "You sound so sure," Mom said.

I was sure. The war was over, Uncle Bob was safe, and his Journey line—which seemed as real and true to me as if I hadn't made it up myself—was strong and long and clear. Besides, hadn't I learned that nothing stayed the same, not even if you wanted it to?

Lisa was worrying about what to wear to Freshman Orientation. It would be too hot, she said, for us to wear our new school clothes. But what if everyone else did?

"How are we supposed to know how to dress?" I wanted to know. "We haven't even been to high school yet. That's the reason we're going to the orientation in the first place."

"To find out how to get dressed?" Mrs. Siegel asked.

"How to dress," Lisa corrected her.

"This is ridiculous!" I cried. "We are not going to the orientation to find out how to dress! We're going to find out about extracurricular activities and to get a tour of the school and to get our lockers assigned and figure out where they are so we'll feel comfortable when school starts next week. Freshman Orientation has nothing to do with clothes!"

"Still," my mother said, "you want to fit in."

"It's impossible to fit in before you've even started!" I exclaimed.

"Nothing's impossible," my mother corrected mildly, "if you put your mind to it."

I could not believe we were talking about clothes. It was too stupid.

"You do want to fit in," Lisa reminded me.

"Of course I want to fit in," I grumbled.

"So what do you think we should wear?" she asked. "Summer clothes or fall clothes?" Lisa had always been stubborn.

We decided to wear our new pleated skirts. Mine was gray and Lisa's was navy blue. And white blouses. And our cardigan sweaters. We would wear bobby sox and black-and-white saddle shoes, as usual.

"We're going to roast," I complained when my mother handed me my sweater.

"You can take it off later," she said.

Of course, people were dressed every which way at the orientation. Dan was wearing a white bedsheet pinned up over one shoulder and a wreath made out of leaves. The sign on his information table said: LATIN CLUB.

There were tables for the German Club, the French

1945

Club, the Future Teachers of America, the Drama
Guild, the Girls' Athletic Association, the Knitters
and Sewers, the Scouts. Debate. Bowling. Tennis.
Chorus. Band. Orchestra. Pep Club. And the Radio
Broadcast Club.

To get to the Radio Broadcast Club, I had to cut
across the crowded cafeteria, through groups of stu-
dents and around other activities tables. Some teachers stood together talking. Several of them were men.
I'd never had a man teacher, and I couldn't help staring.

The familiar-looking girl behind the Radio Broadcast table seemed to be watching me as I came toward
her. When I got closer, I could see that her blue eyes
were bright with what looked like a nice mixture of
mischief and confidence.

"Can anyone join?" I asked.

"Yep," she said.

"What do you do?"

"Everything," she answered. "We write radio
scripts and produce them and broadcast them over
the PA system. And we have performances and com-
pete with kids from other schools. If we win, we move
on to county-wide competitions, and then to state.
We do news and interviews and special features and
plays. We even make up commercials. Everything.
It's the best activity in the school," she said. "If
you're still interested in radio, that is."

Now I knew her! It was the girl from the audition
two summers ago.

"Hi!" I exclaimed.

"Hi," she replied, smiling. She pushed a sign-up

sheet and a pencil toward me. "You'll really like it," she assured me. "We work hard, but we have a lot of fun, too."

I put my name and home room and phone number on the list.

She rolled her eyes. "You're in Mr. Thompson's homeroom?"

I nodded. "And I have him for algebra, too."

"Keep your mouth shut and turn in all your assignments on time," she advised, "and it'll probably be all right."

I nodded again. "Oh, by the way," I said, "did you get a part, that time?"

"I did," she said, smiling. "I got the part of the squirrel."

"The squirrel!"

"It was great," she said. "We had fun. I was really sorry you weren't there."

I thought of telling her, but quickly decided not to. "Well, I'm here now."

"Right!" she said. A couple of people were waiting behind me. She read my name off the sign-up sheet. "See you after school starts, Ellen."

I read her name off her name tag. "Okay, Josie."

I signed up for the Girls' Athletic Association, too. Softball in the fall, volleyball and basketball in the winter, synchronized swimming in the spring.

Then I went over to say hello to Dan. "I'm taking French," I apologized.

"I know," he said, self-consciously straightening his bedsheet.

1945

"But Lisa's taking Latin."

"She already signed up."

"So how come you're wearing a sheet?"

"It's a toga. It's what they wore."

"The Latins?"

"The Romans," he said, glaring at me.

It was stuffy in the crowded cafeteria. I took off my sweater and tied the sleeves around my waist. Then I went outside to wait for Lisa.

I sat down on the grass in front of the school and picked a dandelion with a white head. Perfect for wishing on.

The square old building was two stories high, made out of red brick and surrounded by grass and trees. I'd noticed that the steps inside had grooves worn in them, from all the feet walking up and down over the years, right where I'd be walking now.

All those kids for all those years, trooping up and down the stairs, making friends, going to classes, playing sports, giving plays, having dances in the gym. All of it was old, and all of it was new. All of it was exciting.

My life had changed completely while Uncle Bob was away. He and I were different, and so was everything else. Exactly what I didn't want had happened. Yet I was very glad it did.

I blew the dandelion fluff and watched it scatter, but I didn't make a wish. Hadn't I learned it was impossible to know what to wish for? I was happy now just to wait and see.